Dangerous Love

Lilou DuPont

CRIMSON
ROMANCE
Avon, Massachusetts

This edition published by
Crimson Romance
an imprint of F+W Media, Inc.
10151 Carver Road, Suite 200
Blue Ash, Ohio 45242

www.crimsonromance.com

Copyright © 2012 by Jeryl Parade

ISBN-10: 1-4405-5410-2
ISBN-13: 978-1-4405-5410-0
eISBN-10: 1-4405-5411-0
eISBN-13: 978-1-4405-5411-7

This is a work of fiction.

Names, characters, corporations, institutions, organizations, events, or locales in this novel are either the product of the author's imagination or, if real, used fictitiously. The resemblance of any character to actual persons (living or dead) is entirely coincidental.

Dedication

FOR MY PARENTS

Acknowledgments

The author wishes to thank her family and friends for always believing in her and Crimson Romance for this amazing opportunity.

CHAPTER 1:
BOHEMIAN EYES

"The Look of Bohemian Eyes."

Laura may have created the advertising campaign, but had never actually seen the physical embodiment of Bohemian Eyes—until now. She had just boarded the Czech Air connecting flight from London to Prague, and seated across the aisle was a striking young woman. Charcoal eyeliner dramatically enhanced her already huge blue eyes. She extended her long spindly legs across the bulkhead, in the area illuminated by a singular airplane reading light. Her eyelashes, which were lushly embellished with jet black mascara, cast shadows on her chalky cheeks.

Laura's advertising client had been a large cosmetics conglomerate, whose merchandise lined the shelves of big box retailers and discount drug chains across America. Among the target customers were the young women who worked as cashiers and clerks in these same stores. The marketing promised them escapist nights out on the town as sultry sex goddesses.

Upon arriving in Prague, Laura discovered that many of the young Czech women had "The Look of Bohemian Eyes." The demoiselles could be easily taken for runway models, actresses on the verge of stardom, or unruly heiresses. But from the way they traveled in packs, hauling schoolbooks in stained bags and giggling at the slightest provocations, Laura could tell that they were ordinary girls.

They dressed in the uniform of pencil thin black pants and platform shoes. They wore their cell phones strapped to their wrists like bangle bracelets. Initially, their ubiquitous loveliness was intimidating, but by the end of her first week in her newly adopted city, Laura had successfully managed to replicate the look. Had Laura—while still at the agency—co-opted "The Look" for an audience of American consumers *or* had her vision been exported to and taken hold in this burgeoning capitalist country? She had located the products—in their glittery pink compacts and tubes—in what appeared to be the Eastern European equivalent of a dollar store. Dust had flown in from the streets and coated the plastic wrappings.

The one thing that set Laura apart was her golden hair. It was wild and wavy, whereas the Prague princesses had supremely straight tresses that fell like ironed sheets.

The other (and not so minor) thing setting her apart was her age. At forty-five years old, Laura estimated that she was twice (or possibly three times!) the age of the girls. Her father's girlfriend had once asked Laura how old she was spiritually. Laura had replied without missing a beat, "Sixteen."

Her father had knowingly chimed in. "Laura was a straight-A student and had so many friends in high school," he'd said, seemingly quite happy at the thought of his middle-aged daughter as a sixteen-year-old. He'd gone on to proclaim his true age to be "fifty-something." That was when his business had been at its apex of success and he had made oodles of money.

Paula, the girlfriend, had advised Laura to change her hairstyle and grow up.

"What's your true age?" Laura had asked.

"Me? I'm thirty-nine." Of course, thought Laura. The leopard-patterned aerobics suit, Botox injections, and eyelid surgeries seemed to attest to this.

Admittedly, Laura did not always look or feel young, particularly after working seventy hours in a given week and depriving herself of sleep. What made her seem timeless was that she had held on to her dreams, taking risks and living with the consequences. She was her own person.

In Prague, Laura was also encountering a considerably older

generation of Czech women. Toiling as lavatory room attendants, tram operators, and museum guards, they had fleshy faces and bodies that looked and smelled like sacks of potatoes. They made Laura wonder how one could go from Point A to Point B in the span of twenty years.

Indeed, Laura had gone from Point A to Point B in far less time. Just three months ago, she was a successful advertising executive at an agency in Chicago. Then, the board of directors brought in a man thirteen years her junior to run the place and be her boss. To Laura, the new whippersnapper—with his slicked back hair and overpowering citrus cologne—was all show, lacking her own substance and tireless work ethic. Was it due to her age or because she was a woman that the board had overlooked her for this promotion? Laura suspected that it was neither, that it was base corporate greed that she was unable or unwilling to feed. She suddenly saw that she had sailed right past the high point of her career and was now on an inexorable descent.

She had graduated from the University of Chicago with a BA and an MBA and, in 1984, gone straight to work. Unlike many of her contemporaries, Laura had not taken off time for traveling or studying abroad. Consequently, she had always dreamed of someday living in self-imposed exile in a foreign country. She had read about a Bohemian scene in Prague comprised mainly of English-speaking expatriates from the United States and Great Britain.

Prague was also the birthplace of Franz Kafka, the existential writer with whom Laura shared the same religion—Judaism.

Laura had amassed a large quantity of stock options: First, when her fledgling agency went public and later, at each corporate milestone. She had never exercised any of them. All told, they were worth tens of thousands of dollars. So, right before announcing her resignation, Laura cashed in. She could comfortably live off the profits for close to a year.

In a reversal of Kafka's *The Metamorphosis*, which was about a man who unexpectedly wakes up one day as a repugnant cockroach, Laura went to sleep one night as an agency drone dressed in corporate gray. The next day, she woke up as a liberated damselfly, flapping her fuchsia-spotted wings.

She signed a short-term rental contract, which committed her to three months from May through July. Her new home was a sprawling loft on the top floor of a dilapidated palace. It was sandwiched between much newer Art Nouveau structures on *Jecna*, the central artery through Prague 2. The building dated back to the fifteenth century when radical Hussites had used it as a fort during their religious war against Rome. Grotesque gargoyles stared down at Laura from the high ceiling. They were the first things she saw when she opened her eyes each morning.

Not having brought along any of her own furniture, Laura slept on the floor on a newly purchased mattress. There was a battered Rococo armoire with shelves for her books and a place to hang up her nicer clothes.

Someone had also left behind a Louis XV writing desk. Laura imagined Marie Antoinette with a feathered quill penning the famous words, "Let them eat cake!" while a mob downstairs screamed for her head. Only, that mêlée had occurred in Versailles and Laura was in Prague.

Prague—having emerged from World War II with its gorgeous Gothic architecture largely unscathed—reminded Laura of home. Chicago had weathered disasters, too, and both urban hubs now had blocks of gentrification, with boutiques and brasseries sprouting up like dandelions. The Midwestern city skyline reflected in Lake Michigan had never failed to fill Laura with wonder, and here, the Charles Bridge and Prague Castle illuminated at night and the sparkling Vltava River made her equally awestruck.

It was a beautiful day in late May. She took her time getting ready to go out. From across her loft, she observed her reflection in a gilt-framed mirror. It hung over a barren fireplace that was, according to her landlord, unusable. Laura decided she had the appearance of a Czech-Chicagoan hybrid. She wore the zipper-less black pants and transparent white blouse favored by 90 percent of the young female population of Prague. Further mimicking their style, Laura left most of her shirt unbuttoned, revealing her cleavage and the top of her lacy nude colored bra. But her carefree blonde locks and open, expectant face gave away that she was an American. You can take the girl out of the heartland, Laura mused, but you can't take the heart out of the girl.

CHAPTER 2:
PRAGUE DREAMING

Outside, the air was balmy and the sun glistened. It was nearly two in the afternoon. Laura had not yet completely adjusted to the seven-hour time difference, but she felt obliged to do something worthwhile to make up for her late start. An exhibition had just opened at a gallery in her neighborhood. It had the intriguing yet foreboding title, "Hasidic Drawings from The Holocaust."

Hasidic men were known for their black hats, long coats, and spiraling, unshaven side curls. Moreover, Hasidic Jews were deeply mystical. Laura had always been drawn to their cliquish religiosity, yet knew she did not belong. They would shun her secularism.

The curatorial notes were in three languages, Czech, English, and German. Laura skimmed past the historic details until she reached the final sentence. "In keeping with the life affirming precepts of Hasidism—, the works of this exhibition were selected for their optimism."

Laura spun around and took in all of the exuberant imagery. It was true. Tragic portrayals of the doomed and the deceased were nowhere to be found.

She felt a twinge of suspicion. Could this presentation be a new form of Holocaust denial propaganda? As an obvert ploy to discourage Laura from traveling abroad, her dad had warned that anti-Semitism was running rampant in Europe. Europeans, he had said, hated the Jews. Well, she would see for herself.

The exhibition was small and she completed her viewing of the homogenous works in less than ten minutes. Laura purchased a book for 50 *Korunas* and stepped outside. Surprisingly, dark clouds now hung low in the sky. She had only gone one block when they burst open, pelting her with rain.

She ran to the nearest refuge, which happened to be the Globe Bookstore and Café, a hangout popular with Yanks and Brits. The place was packed with people who were also fleeing from the sudden storm. Laura spotted an empty table and sat down with her cappuccino.

Across the room, a man was using paper napkins to dry his black leather jacket. He seemed to be her age or a few years older. His brown hair was layered and covered his collar. Could he be an American? Laura noted the elegant style of his messenger bag. The attaché was decidedly of this continent and not "Made in the U.S.A."

There was an extra chair at her table. Laura opened her book and tried to read about a strong-willed, ten-year-old girl who had survived a Nazi labor camp. In spite of the compelling content, Laura could not concentrate. She peered up from the pages and spotted the man again. He was holding a steaming cup and staring at her from across the room. Their eyes met and he started to walk toward her.

"Is someone sitting here?"

He has a British accent, noted Laura. The man was not from the United States.

"No."

"May I?"

"Sure. Go ahead."

The man sat down. She sipped on her hot drink. All she got was foamy milk. She pretended to be reading, but was really watching him douse a satchel of Earl Grey tea into the cup of scorching water. She was feeling hot herself. Inexplicably, the messy vapors were reminding her of her own body heat in the moments before orgasm!

Let it go, Laura told herself. He's just a guy taking the one empty seat.

She took another sip. This time, she got a gulp of rich espresso. The strong caffeine jolted her. She gazed up at the man. Strands of her hair hung in her face. She supposed she should get a haircut one of these days. Her hair dipped into her coffee and came back out with foamy milk stuck to the ends.

"Oops," she said and smiled at him.

The man shocked her by brushing the hair out of her eyes. One of the strands stuck to her lip gloss.

"Are you an American?" he asked her.

"You can tell?"

"Yes."

"How can you tell?" She knew it was completely obvious, but wanted to expand the conversation.

"The book you are reading. It is in English."

"And my accent."

"Yes, your accent. It must have been the way you said, 'Oops.'"

"That was a dead giveaway."

"Yes. And . . . I find that Americans are fascinated by the complexities surrounding the Holocaust. Much more so than Europeans. The title of your book intrigues me."

Laura looked at the cover. "You are not, by any chance, Hasidic?"

He laughed. "No, of course not."

"I didn't think so."

"I am an art dealer and have been meaning to check out that exhibit."

"The gallery is right down the street."

"Yes, I know. If you had not already gone, I would take you there."

Laura felt him press his knees into hers beneath the table. Was the gesture accidental or intentional? Her reflex was to pull away from this unknown man, but she did not want her Eastern European adventure to be about missed opportunities. So she kept her knees in place, touching his.

"What's your name?" she asked.

"Byron."

"Like the poet Lord Byron?"

"Yes, that's right. My father admired all of the romantic poets, Wordsworth, Shelley, Keats, and Rilke—"

"Rilke? Rilke was German."

"Yes, I know, though he was born right here in Prague. And last, but not least, Lord Byron. He named me after the most wayward of them all. What is your name?"

"Laura."

"Lady Laura. It is a pleasure to meet you." He gallantly lifted her hand and kissed it. As he smiled, the lines around his blue-green eyes crinkled. Laura observed that they were not nearly as deep as the white creases in his black leather jacket.

"Thank you," she said. "It's nice meeting you, too."

"Are you sure you are not First Lady Laura Bush?"

"No, no." They both burst out laughing. He let go of her hand. She thought briefly of the United Kingdom's Prime Minister, Tony Blair, and how, in her opinion, he was quite sexy, despite their two countries' alliance in an unpopular war. Perhaps she would have her chance with her own alluring Brit. "I am definitely not Laura Bush," she added.

"If not the Holocaust exhibit, then perhaps there is something else we can do together."

"That would be nice." Laura swilled the last drops of her coffee.

"Would you like to go for a short walk?" He pushed aside his mostly full cup of tea.

"I'd love to."

They left the café. Once outside, they realized that they both had had temporary amnesia. The rain was coming down furiously. This was going to be a very "short walk" indeed. They dashed across the slick cobblestones. Byron removed his jacket and held it over the two of them. Thunder bellowed.

"My apartment!" Laura called out and led the way. They ran up the half dozen steps to her building and Laura pushed open the door to the foyer. "I'm on the fourth floor," she said.

Her loft had a picture window overlooking the street. Laura had left it open earlier in the day to let in the warm air, and now a puddle of water soaked the wooden planks. Byron let his damp jacket drop to the floor with a thud. He whisked her to the window.

"Do you know about the Prague tradition of throwing dissidents out of windows?" He tentatively pushed her.

She had read about this medieval practice, known as defenestration, in the "Prague Eccentricities" sidebar in her guidebook. "What will you do to me?" she said, feigning innocence.

"Don't worry. I won't hurt you."

The torrent of rain had relented to a mist. Sunshine punctured an immense gray cloud that loomed near the horizon. Above it, the sky resembled cotton candy, swirling in orchid, pink, and aqua.

"You have a beautiful view."

"Thanks."

Byron looked away from the window and at Laura. "But not as beautiful as the view *I* have of *you*."

He kissed her on the mouth. Laura felt a rush of passion. This type of spontaneous encounter would never have happened to her in Chicago, due to that city's geographic sprawl and impersonal ethos. In compact, quixotic Prague, anything was possible.

Byron stepped back and twirled a piece of her hair. He tugged and released it. He led her to the center of the room and pulled her down with him on the mattress. The flaring bottoms of her otherwise skintight pants were drenched. He stripped them off her.

She was wearing her sheer, pastel pink underwear. Her brown pubic hair was visible from beneath the fabric. Just as she thought they might be moving too fast, he hesitated. He stared at her with admiration and without touching. But she longed to be touched!

He reached for her bare thighs and flipped her over. He gently stroked her buttocks. Laura shivered with delight. It was unbelievable. It had been a long time, but had it ever been like this? He raised his hand and held it above her ass for several seconds. Then, he slapped her.

"Ouch!" Laura cried out, surprised. She wondered if she had pronounced the word "ouch"—as she had the word "oops"—with an American accent.

"Did you like that?"

"It was not what I was expecting."

"I know." He tore off her panties and pulled down his trousers. He stood on his knees. He was wearing blue and white striped boxers and had a huge bulge. "Perhaps you were expecting this."

"Perhaps . . . " said Laura. His cock peered out from the top of the boxer shorts. She kneeled also and faced Byron. She pulled at the elastic waistband, providing her new buddy with some breathing room. It leaped toward her.

"Lord Byron!" Laura exclaimed. "It's nice to meet you."

"Enchanted," Byron said in a gruff voice.

She gave Lord Byron a squeeze. Byron closed his eyes and moaned. He removed his shorts and threw Laura down on the bed. He separated her legs and positioned himself above her, for immediate entry.

What was she doing? Had she made a big mistake? Byron was essentially a stranger. Laura felt catapulted back in time to high school, torn between wanting to stop and not wanting to be labeled a cock tease.

Reflexively, she clamped her legs together. She was extremely wet! Her juices flowed between her thighs.

"What's wrong?"

"I don't know. We just met."

"When I saw you sitting like that in the Globe, I knew I had to have you."

"Sitting like what?" Laura was genuinely confused.

"Like so fragile and intense. Your hair was wet." He was above her and held some of it in his hands. "It still is."

"I noticed you first. When you came in."

"Not when I came in. Your back was to me then. I saw your golden hair down your thin body as you went to your table with your coffee and your book."

"So you saw me first."

"I admit that that initial snapshot of you triggered something physiological in me—"

"Like what? Did you get hard?"

"I did. But it was not until I saw your face that I knew I had to act on it."

"I knew I wanted you, too."

"Then, there is nothing to be afraid of."

"I'm not so sure," Laura said. "Do you have a condom?"

"A condom?"

"Yes. We don't really know each other. I have one." In fact, she had a dozen of them. Laura got up and went to the eighteenth century writing desk. Thank you, Louis XV, she thought. There was nothing in the shallow center drawer but felt tipped markers and an unopened box of condoms.

She ripped apart the package and grabbed one in its foil casing. She returned to Byron and helped him put it on.

He unbuttoned her blouse and slid it from her shoulders. He kissed the tops of her breasts. He reached behind her and unhooked her skimpy bra. It dropped in the space between them. She was completely naked at last.

He pulled on and twisted her nipples. The sensation traveled right down to her clitoris. He embraced her, gliding his hands past her narrow waist and to her hips. As she arched her back, he relocated her opening. This time, she allowed him to slide right in. They landed on her mattress, with Byron above and Laura below.

And then he pounded her. She was shocked by how rough he was and how much she liked it!

He stopped momentarily and looked her in the eyes. "I apologize."

"It's fine. It's more than fine."

"No. It's not very gentlemanly of me. It's going to be very quick." And with that, he shoved himself deep inside her, cried out, and came. As he did, he clutched her hair and collapsed on top of her.

He stayed that way without moving or speaking. Eventually, he muttered, "I'm sorry."

"Don't worry about it. You're great."

He did not budge. "If you don't mind, I would like to stay here for all of eternity."

After some time, his cock shrank and slipped out of her hole.

He rolled off her. He tied a knot in the top of the condom so that nothing would leak out. Leaning on his side, Byron stared at her face and stroked her hair. "Your hair is dry now."

"But I'm not," she quipped.

"Did you come?"

Laura shook her head no.

"What a self-absorbed bloke I am. How will I ever make it up to you?" Answering his own question, he planted kisses on her belly and worked his way down to her V. He flicked his tongue on precisely the right spot. He was suddenly so amazing and so sweet. With each tap, her triangle vibrated like the musical instrument of the same name.

The rhythmic strokes intensified to a lashing. She begged and cried out for more. He gripped the tops of her thighs. A surge of desire exploded from deep within her. She screamed again. Her legs thrashed about, despite his clutches. Her torso propelled in the air and to him. Her voice was belting out the high notes of an opera singer. Laura was sure that all of Prague could hear her orgasm.

It was growing dark outside. They drifted off to sleep for what felt like a few minutes. The passionate yelps of another woman woke them. It sounded as if she were in the same building with her window also flung wide open. Was it possible that she too was experiencing shared magic? Or was the other woman—as Laura had been up until now—alone?

"You inspired her," he said.

"*We* inspired her. Or them," she giggled, snuggling up against him.

"I did not hear a man."

"Not every man is as vocal as you."

"Do I talk too much? Or should I say, do I grunt too much?"

"I like listening to you. You have such a cute British accent."

"That's funny. I'm not British."

"You're not? What are you?"

"German."

Laura froze in his embrace. "You are? You don't have a German accent."

"I know. My accent is ambiguous. It's from going to Swiss boarding schools."

Huh? Like I should have known this, thought Laura. "Oh."

"Where are you from?" Byron asked.

"Chicago."

"I mean, originally. Where is your family from? Everyone in the States is from somewhere else, unless Native American or a Daughter of the American Revolution. I rather doubt that you are either."

"I'm Jewish. I didn't know you were German."

"Does that bother you?"

"A little."

"What the Nazis did to the Jews was unconscionable. I have always wanted to discuss the war with my father, but the subject was off limits."

"How old was he during the war?"

"He was old enough."

"What does that mean?"

"He was a teenager. Like most boys of his generation, he was in the Hitler Youth."

Laura felt a wrenching in her gut. She had just slept with the son of a *Nazi*.

How had this happened? She had allowed herself to be infiltrated by the son of a disciple of the master of death. Now there were just two degrees of separation between Laura and #%@! It was too despicable even to contemplate. Guilt overwhelmed her. She had betrayed her people, specifically the 6 million murdered Jews.

Laura could not help but think, *This is what happens when you spread your legs after knowing someone for all of one hour, Slut Girl.*

Remarkably, she was still in his arms.

"I'm not taking this very well," she told him. "I think you should leave."

"Are you sure?"

"Yes."

He quickly dressed. Laura watched him zip up his trousers, walk across the room, and open the door. He turned to look at her. "I do understand, Laura, but if you should change your mind—"

"I don't know how I can change my mind about this."

He left, closing the door behind him. They had not even exchanged cell phone numbers or e-mail addresses. For the first time in Prague, she felt stabbed with loneliness. Her loft seemed eerily empty.

*

In the days that followed, Laura perceived Prague as a haunted city. She visited the house in which Kafka had grown up. It was now a jewel of a museum, at the edge of the Jewish Ghetto. His youthful writings, along with photos of a once-prospering Kafka family, were on display. Laura learned that during the Holocaust, the Nazis had deported Franz's sisters on Yom Kippur. All three women perished.

Next stop was the Prague Jewish Museum. The Nazis had confiscated Jewish artifacts with the intent of showing them off as the spoils of war, in a sick and twisted tribute to an extinct race.

Laura stood in reverence at a shrine, dedicated to the memory of those slaughtered in the camps. German-speaking tourists swarmed her. They gawked and pointed to the memorial plaques. "Auschwitz," one of them said in a stage whisper.

They were making her feel like the bug of *The Metamorphosis*.

She was a speck among these Aryan giants. *Hah! No one can crush the Jews! They must think of us as mutants, able to resist their harshest pesticides*, Laura speculated. *What does Byron think?*

The Old New Synagogue was just around the corner, according to her map. Laura's mind was reeling. Praying or sitting in a sanctuary might help her regain inner peace. Policemen were stationed at the synagogue's entrance. An imposing iron fence encircled the temple. Worship times were posted on a sign. There was a service scheduled for 6 p.m. Laura looked at her watch. It was 5:45 p.m. She was anxious to go in.

"It's closed," one of the guards told her in English. People here automatically—and accurately—assumed she was American. Yet they did not quickly jump to the next correct conclusion, that she was Jewish.

"But there's a service at six. I'd like to go inside."

"The synagogue closes to the public at five thirty."

"But I'm not here for a tour. I'm here to pray."

"I will need to see your passport."

Laura handed it to him. After inspecting each blank and unstamped page of her passport, the officer let her in. She was directed to the "women's section."

In Orthodox congregations, women were prohibited to pray alongside the men. A *mechitzah* (a trellis or an opaque partition) separated the sexes or the females sat in a balcony. At the Old New Synagogue, this concept was taken to the extreme, with the women relegated to the outer lobby. Folding aluminum chairs faced a wall. Round holes had been randomly carved in the barricade. The design reminded Laura of a cruise ship. She took a seat and looked through one of the portholes.

She could see the men in their skull caps, milling about and *kipitzing* (chatting). Finally, they settled down and recited the opening prayer. While Laura was familiar with these Hebrew words, she could barely hear the male voices.

There were three other women in the lobby. They wore heavy, floor length skirts. They busied themselves by placing fish pieces and crackers on a silver tray.

As it was May, Laura knew that the week's Torah portion might be *Kedoshim,* which translated as "The Holy Ones." It included the Ten Commandments along with passages banning specific sexual relations (between a father and his daughter-in-law or a son and his stepmother). Laura wanted to look up to see if there was anything unlawful about sleeping with the Biblical equivalent of the son of a Nazi. It might be phrased as a "descendent of the destroyer of the Jews."

There were prayer books on the empty chairs, but no Bibles. She opened one of them. Its pages were rippled and yellow. The book could have been 150 years old. There was no Czech or English, just tiny Hebrew lettering without the vowels.

When the service concluded, Laura left without speaking to anyone or sharing in the light meal. She felt too out of place. She ran away from the Jewish Quarter. What was she doing here? What was she doing in the Czech Republic, a Second World country that had endured Nazi occupation and then Soviet domination? Was it possible that in Prague she had met her soul mate? Yet how could her soul merge with the son of a Nazi?

She headed toward the river. It was dusk and warm tungsten light emanated from one of the waterfront buildings. Laura saw that it was the Bohemian Glass Museum and that it was open until eight p.m. tonight.

After paying the nominal entrance fee, she proceeded to a rectangular room. The white walls smelled of fresh paint. The glass display cases were squeaky clean. There were bottles, jugs, and vases in a dazzling array of shapes and colors. The effect was kaleidoscopic. Laura was enraptured. For the first time since she had set out today, she felt serene.

She continued to a smaller, square room where the glass formations were of jungle animals, waterfowl, and other creatures. Laura noticed a gold starfish with purple tips. And then she saw *him*.

The sight of him took her breath away. In a city of more than 1 million people, what were the chances that she would run into Byron? *It must be fate.*

He was studying a figurine. It was a blue-green seahorse. The glass was the same color as his eyes.

Her heart was beating wildly. He looked up and saw her.

She blurted out without thinking. "I'm sorry I kicked you out."

He smiled broadly. "Did you miss me? I missed you."

"Yes, I did. I did miss you."

She had been in a daze since he had left. Now that she had uttered these words, she knew them to be true.

The faint lines around his mouth were obscured by scruffiness. He must not have shaven that morning or the day before that. Why not? Had he been similarly distraught over losing her?

"I understand how you feel, Laura. But I was not the one in the Hitler Youth."

"I know that."

"Good."

While Laura "got" that Byron was not guilty of the sins of his father, she felt anxiety about being so close to someone who had been so close to someone who had been a Nazi. And yet . . .

"This is such a beautiful museum."

"It is near closing time. Would you like to go for a walk?"

"Hey, at least it's not raining."

"Let's try again, Laura."

He took her hand as they left the gallery and crossed the black-and-white checkerboard floor. It was dark outside. They strolled along the river. The air was especially hot and humid. Laura relished the way her lightweight skirt brushed against her bare legs above her knees.

She suddenly wished that this night in Prague would never

end. Byron talked about his father. "He was in a club with other German boys and girls. They hiked and sang nationalistic songs and played games."

"What kinds of games?"

"Kids' games at first. Later, they were fiercely competitive to prepare my father for real combat. My grandmother told me that by the time he was eleven or twelve, she rarely saw him. He slept away from home on most nights. At thirteen, he was in the army."

"Thirteen? That's so young to enlist!"

"Laura, my father did not volunteer. He was conscripted. He had no choice."

"Of course not," Laura quietly agreed. "He was not an adult." Or was he? Thirteen was the age when a Jewish boy becomes a man and a Jewish girl becomes a woman, assuming all moral responsibilities of adulthood. Her own Bat Mitzvah had taken place in a huge synagogue in suburban Chicago. She had worn an A-line herringbone dress (suitable for a new client presentation, even then), a size 30AA bra, nylon stockings, and black patent leather shoes. Laura and her mother had shopped for the whole kit and caboodle at Lord & Taylor. Standing before hundreds of congregants and guests, confidently chanting in Hebrew and leading them in responsive reading, Laura had undoubtedly felt like an adult.

The Nazis had indoctrinated Byron's father and thousands of other German boys at this same impressionable age to worship Adolf Hitler.

"I worry that I will never know what he did in the war."

"Do you really want to know?"

"Yes. As much as I dread hearing the truth."

They approached the gaily lit Charles Bridge. It was teeming with tourists, beggars, and street musicians. "What do you say, Laura? Shall we be brave? Shall we go across?"

"Yes. Let's do it."

They were walking in the direction away from her apartment.

She felt untethered and free. Byron put his arm around her, shielding her from the boisterous mob.

When they reached the land on the other side, he said, "I want to show you something."

He brought her to a secluded area underneath the bridge. They sat down on a grassy patch. They watched the waves lap up to the pebbled shore and the city lights shimmer on the water's surface. When they both got tired, they lay down in each other's arms and stayed that way until the sun came up the following day.

CHAPTER 3:
GARDEN OF EARTHLY DELIGHTS

Predawn was damp and chilly. Noises from the masses of people on the bridge did not fade until the wee hours. They slept, using his black leather jacket as a blanket.

The sun warmed her back. Their arms and legs were tangled up in a web. When Laura opened her eyes, she saw *his* eyes. They were closed. His eyelids and lashes fluttered. The sun was low on the horizon. She desperately needed to use a bathroom.

Byron opened his eyes and said, "Good morning, my lovely. Don't go anywhere. I'll be right back." He unscrambled himself from her and got up.

Laura watched him go to a grouping of wildflowers, unzip his jeans, and pull out his watering hose. Impolitely, she did not look away as he sprayed the terrain. He seemed so relaxed and unselfconscious. The slanted rays of the sun blazed through the sprinkling arc.

It was her turn and not a moment too soon. Watching Byron had made the water pressure build up in her faucet. She shoved up her skirt and squatted over the stones, mud, and blades of grass. Her urine gushed out. Unlike his stream, hers was completely unfocused, splashing her ankles and calves and even her thighs. The release was absolutely satisfying.

"What a nice morning ritual," she said.

"I know of a better one," replied Byron, looking her up and down. Fortunately, she had not worn any makeup the previous day, which meant that her face was smudge free. But her hair had to be a wreck.

He pulled her toward him. He kissed her hungrily on the lips. He moved his hands beneath her shirt and felt her breasts.

"I love your body." His cock was hard and demanding. It jutted out from his open fly. He lifted her up. She wrapped her legs around his hips. As he held her in the air, she was positioned above his erection. Together, they located her opening. He pushed in.

He carried her away from the piss puddles. Her body jiggled along with the bounce of his steps. He returned her to their makeshift bed and carefully lowered her to the ground. Laura was amazed that they did all of this while they were attached. It was as if they were supposed to be attached.

"I have never wanted anyone the way I want you." He said this in a husky whisper while stroking her hair and kissing her neck. Laura was flooded with excitement. She felt exactly the same way.

He inched out of her hole, raised her arms above her head, and pinned her to the mossy earth. With his garden tool, he grazed her outer petals. He plunged back inside of her. He grimaced above her as he moved hard and fast and deep. She felt his hot semen shoot into her. As it expanded, her flesh soaked it up like a sponge. They held each other, cocoon style. Laura loved this. Then she realized there had been no condom this time. They had forgotten all about safe sex. Laura knew what they had just had: Dangerous sex.

He pulled out and climbed off her. "I am going to Bratislava."

"What? When?"

"Today."

He's leaving? *Now?* Sex was risky in more ways than one. It was the proverbial fuck and run, articulated in the song of the same name by fellow Chicagoan, Liz Phair. This had happened to Laura more than once in her near thirty years of consenting adulthood. No matter. It always made Laura feel like shit.

"What's in Bratislava?"

"Not what's in Bratislava, but *who* is in Bratislava. An up and coming sculptor," Byron said. "I am going there to check out his work."

Laura was relieved to hear the word "his."

"I may sign him as a client," Byron continued. "He's at the

center of a new movement, the Retrograde Soviets."

"I've never heard of them."

"They are artists who are too young to remember Stalin and the Old Guard. Their work is nostalgic for totalitarianism. Can you believe that?"

"It sounds fascinating." She was trying to hide her disappointment that he was leaving.

"It is. Would you like to come with me?"

"To Bratislava?" She felt thrilled.

"Yes. Have you ever been there?"

"No. Never. I have been to only three European cities, Paris, London, and Prague."

"Then we must expand your horizons. Bratislava is a great place to start. The Slovakian people love Americans, especially your fascist president, George Bush."

While Laura on her home soil might agree with this cavalier assessment of her nation's leader, in Europe, and especially given Byron's familial background, she was offended. Better not go there.

"I would love to come," she said.

They agreed to meet at the train station at eleven in the morning. The trip from Prague to Bratislava would last approximately three hours, Byron told her.

*

She walked home alone. She came upon a poster for the Czech National Ballet Company stapled to an electrical pole. A ballerina, her tutu awash in pastels, her slippers scuffed, was on her tiptoes. The imagery reminded Laura of her own balancing act. She was teetering between falling head over heels in love with Byron and descending into contempt for his German heritage. The poster was signed, "Jolene."

She gazed across the street. A young woman with flowing brown hair was watching her. Remembering how she had slept, pissed, and fucked in her clothes, Laura turned away and headed home.

CHAPTER 4:
JOLENE

What does that woman think of my poster? Jolene had gone out early to take out the trash before jumping in the shower.

She guessed that the transfixed onlooker was an American. Her crinkly blonde hair and stressful stare were strong indicators. Europeans similarly engrossed in thought were hard to read. Jolene had discovered this fact upon her arrival several months ago at the modern Prague airport. Not to mention the woman's high platform athletic shoes, suitable for endless hours of strolling unknown streets. Jolene remembered seeing them on Zappos.com for a mere 125 USD. She was obviously a tourist, geared up for some serious sightseeing.

At seven in the morning?

The blonde woman furled her eyebrows, as if trying to penetrate with x-ray vision the years and layers of plastered over, weathered posters. Could she be a potential benefactor, admiring the elegance of Jolene's drawing?

"Who is this *Zso-een?*" Jolene could hear the woman asking the uppity administrator of the Prague Ballet Company. In Jolene's fantasy, the woman knowingly mispronounced her name with a French accent for dramatic effect. "I demand the 411." After having purchased a stack of Jolene's canvases and carting them back to the United States, the woman would announce to her equally discriminating, moneyed, art-world friends: "I have discovered this amazing young artist. She needs no last name, as the great ones never do. She goes by *Zso-een.*" Leo would love that. Yeah, right. Her boyfriend abhorred pretensions. He called her Joey.

Go up and talk to her. This can be your chance for fame and fortune. But how likely was that? Were those grass stains on her skirt? Really. If she were homeless, wouldn't she be even more covered in dirt?

Joey was crossing the street when she remembered she was holding a garbage bag. It was jangling with beer bottles from the night before. Leave it to Leo and his buddies. What kind of first impression was this? *Lose the trash!* She raced to the nearest receptacle and tossed the bag, making an easy basket and shattering the quietude of the street. She sprinted back.

By then, the woman had left. Jolene felt an inexplicable sense of loss. She tried to convince herself that the mystery woman was a high-priced call girl from Estonia. That country had free wi-fi and was reeling in cash. Its capital city of Tallin was a destination for raucous young men on holiday break. A prostitute there could easily afford and acquire a footlocker of couture shoes.

Jolene knew in her heart of hearts that this was not true. She was spinning a web of fabrication. She had experienced a pull from this stranger and Jolene was always right about such things.

Her mother, the proto-feminist who had advanced to the top of her legal profession using sharply honed analytic skills, dismissed Joey's purported sixth sense.

Back in their dreary apartment, their bed was still unmade and rumpled. Leo was in the shower. He had been in there for a good half hour. Jolene was used to his morning ritual of lathering up and shaving his head. She could picture the droplets of water beading up on his silken ivory skin.

The thought of his wet rippling physique aroused her. She eagerly removed her clothes and got ready to join him. She heard him turn off the faucet. Leo emerged from the fog wearing nothing but a towel around his waist.

She stood naked, facing Leo. Girls her height (five feet, seven inches) and her age (twenty-five) thought they were supposed to weigh 105 pounds. Thankfully, Leo had no desire to be with a paper doll. Jolene had been a jock from middle school through college and continued to be muscular.

She was grateful to her mom that she did not have a body image problem. It was one of the good things that her mother had instilled in her.

Title IX had been breakthrough legislation, enacted long ago in the 1970s. It guaranteed equal funding for both girls and boys scholastic athletics. Her mother had endlessly complained, "It wasn't like that for me. I just missed out."

True, it wasn't. But Joey, a star point guard in high school, knew that her bookish, revolutionary mother had not cared one whit for sports in her day.

And neither did Joey, as Leo came toward her, placed his palms on her bare ass, and let the towel fall away.

CHAPTER 5:
LAURA'S DILEMMA

Laura's apartment building had been painted a garish lavender hue. From the street, it was hard to miss. According to the rental agent, squatters had done the renovations in a fit of democratic ebullience, immediately following the collapse of Communism. That had been many years ago and now the purple paint was peeling off, leaving in its wake large swatches of proletarian brown.

Laura thought of her temporary home as a playhouse. The sun was low on the horizon and the front steps were suffused in a pale yellow light. She headed upstairs and unlocked the door to her loft.

She saw the mattress on the floor where Byron had pounded her. Missing was the condom, which she had reluctantly scooped up and flushed down the toilet after she had told him to leave. All of that had occurred three days ago.

The windows, where Byron had teasingly threatened to push her, were sealed shut. They muffled the everyday street noises—the squealing tram and the trash gnawing truck—from down below. The glass panes were smeared with grease and therefore opaque. Laura was able to strip shamelessly naked in front of them.

In her bare feet, she moved across the rutted wooden planks. The flooring was centuries old. Perhaps a young Czech countess had been taken down on this same base (as Laura had) by an invader Hun. Was such a scenario even historically plausible? Laura had no idea.

Standing in the shower, she let the water cascade over her. She moved the bar of soap between her thighs. It was handmade and organic. She had purchased it at Lush, the ecologically conscious bath and beauty store. All of the products had cutesy names.

This one—pretty in pink and sugary smelling—was called Rock Star. She rubbed the corner between her intimate folds. She then recalled how the Nazis had made soap out of the remains of their Jewish victims. She replaced the soap on the tub ledge.

She pointed the shower nozzle upward at her sex and let the water pulsate between her crevices. How she loved these European contraptions! She sprayed herself until long after she was clean. The Nazis had told the Jews that they were going to the disinfection showers. There they were gassed to death. She hung up the shower hose and turned off the water.

By 1944 and 1945, Germany had lost many of its adult soldiers and depended on young boys to do the fighting. Had the Hitler Youth been dispatched to guard the camps? Had Byron's father ever switched on the noxious fumes?

She dried her body with a luxurious white towel. Laura had allowed Byron to penetrate her innermost space. She was appalled that his father had been a young Nazi, but it was too late to turn back. They had not even left for Bratislava and their journey had already begun.

CHAPTER 6:
EURO RAIL

Two hours later, Byron met Laura at the train station. The lobby was grand and ornate. Upstairs on the platform, there were signs that read "*Praha*" ("Prague" in Czech). Byron saw that the first two seats of the railcar were empty. He took Laura's hand and led her there.

"Have you ever been on the Euro Rail?" he asked.

"No, this is my first time."

"You are in for an adventure," he said boldly.

"Why? I've been on trains before. Commuter trains in Chicago."

"You have never taken the train with *me*."

"What's so special about taking the train with you?"

"You'll see." He could not wait to show her.

The conductor punched their tickets. The train left the station. Byron looked out the window. As they pulled away from the central environs of Prague, drab, prefab housing of the Soviet era whizzed by.

A gray haze obscured their view. It was smog. Frigid air blew out of the ceiling vents. Laura was wearing a short, floral printed dress. The tops of her thighs were dotted with goose bumps. Byron covered her legs with his black leather jacket.

It rested heavily on her legs. The sleeves were pricked with pinholes.

"What kind of jacket is this?" Laura asked.

"It belonged to my father. I tore off the swastika and the other emblems."

"This is what your father wore when he was in the Hitler Youth? Shouldn't it be a lot smaller? You told me he was a boy."

"He grew into it, so to speak."

"What does that mean?"

"At first, the jacket was too big for him. I imagine that he was swimming in it. By the end of World War II, it was a perfect fit."

"Are you saying that he grew into being a Nazi?"

"He refuses to discuss the war. As I have told you, the subject is off limits."

She was continuing to inspect the leather bomber. Where the patches had been, the fabric was shiny black and appeared new, in contrast to the rest of the jacket, which was faded to a light gray. "The weather is warm. It's May. Why are you wearing it now?"

"I always wear it. I am attached to this jacket."

"Why?"

He had never been able to explain this. For Laura, he would try. "Maybe wearing it brings me closer to my father."

She rested her head against his shoulder. Her hair was still damp from her morning shower. He fondled her blonde curls.

*

Laura felt herself getting wet from the small action of Byron lightly touching her hair. When he stroked her neck, she grew even more aroused. She wanted him to kiss her passionately, to ravage and caress her everywhere. Yet he did none of this.

Did he know what a powerful impact he had on her? He had to know. She was growing frustrated beyond belief. Maybe it was his Nazi past. No. He was not a Nazi. He was the son of a Nazi. Maybe his father had trained him (subconsciously, of course) in the art of mental manipulation, skills that could be adapted and applied to sexual torture. Byron slid his hand between her thighs.

"Oh!" Laura cried out. There were other passengers in the railcar, but Byron did not seem to care. Presumably, he knew what they could (or could not) get away with on a train in Europe. He glided his hand past her panties and went right for her gash.

"Oh!" she cried out again. Their railcar entered a tunnel while another train blasted by them, gusting in the opposite direction.

They were engulfed by a deep rumble and darkness. Byron sheltered her in his arms, protecting her from any danger. When they emerged from the tunnel, they were overwhelmed by sunlight.

He covered her eyes with his hands, as if blindfolding her. Finally, he kissed her on the mouth. His fingers separated, allowing in a burst of white light. It was ordinary daylight and she was on a midday train, somewhere in Bohemia. Yet it was more like being on Space Mountain at Disney World. Would Byron get the reference?

The tip of his tongue entered her mouth and teased her. She wanted it down her throat. From the tacky seat, she lifted up her buttocks, struggling to be as close to him as possible.

He reached inside the low, scooped out neckline of her peasant dress. He attacked her nipples, brushing them back and forth. Laura was so stimulated she wanted to scream. He restrained her by kissing her again. Now his tongue aggressively explored her. She sucked on it, wanting much, much more.

*

She's ready, thought Byron. He cast her down on his lap and covered her head with his jacket. She was in a tent. Her hair was splayed across his tensed thighs. He felt his erection pressing uncomfortably against his pants. He wanted Laura more than he had ever wanted anyone. Byron undid the top button of his trousers. Laura pulled down the zipper.

Lord Byron leaped out of the opening of his boxer shorts. Freedom! At last! With her supple lips, Laura took the shaft into her warm, wet mouth. *Oh . . .* Byron thought. *Thank you.*

She sucked on his cock, bobbing her head up and down. Each long, satiny movement, each suctioning squeeze brought him new and intense pleasure. She knew exactly what he wanted and how he wanted it, often before he did. She was a treasure, *his* treasure.

That first sighting of Laura—of her long, golden hair cascading down her back, her thin waist, the curve of her hips—flashed before him. He imagined taking her from behind and ramming her.

Hot come gushed out of him and into her mouth. He felt her swallow. That's my girl, that's my Laura, he thought, as she gobbled up his semen. She was gorgeous and *smart*, too! There would be no incriminating traces of what they—the three co-conspirators, L., B., and L.B.—had just done.

Laura rolled off his lap and straightened up. Byron felt the icy air against his skin. Lord Byron was exposed! "*Scheisse,*" he said and quickly zipped up his fly.

A train conductor was hovering over the two of them.

Oh, no, thought Byron.

"When we get to Vienna," the conductor said, "you're getting off."

*

Laura looked up. She hoped—absurdly and futilely—that what the conductor meant was this: When they got to Vienna, it would be Laura's turn to get off, to have the "Big O."

But she knew that they were in Big Trouble, the "Big T."

CHAPTER 7:
VIENNA

"Wien! Zien minuten!" the conductor announced to the passengers on the train. Laura was sitting upright. The notorious Nazi jacket covered Byron's lap. She wiped any telltale drops of semen from her lips.

"What did he say?"

"We'll be there in ten minutes."

"And then what?"

"We get off. I hope that is all. Think of it this way, Laura. It's another adventure on our way to Bratislava."

"How far are we from Bratislava?"

"About sixty kilometers to the west," Byron said. She was not sure what that meant in miles. It sounded far, but Laura knew a kilometer was shorter than a mile.

"Less than an hour away," he added.

The conductor did not budge from his position at the head of the car, guarding the two of them. He made a call from his mobile phone and began belting out official sounding words in German. She recognized the word, *"frau,"* which she knew meant woman. He must be talking about her. She was starting to think of him as *Das Kommandant.* She imagined him as a Nazi spitting out the word, *"Juden,"* while prodding terrified Jewish females, huddled together in a cattle car that would deliver them to their deaths, to "The Final Solution."

Meanwhile, Byron was surreptitiously moving his hands under the jacket. Laura knew that he was placing Lord Byron back inside his pants.

What will happen to us in Vienna? Laura wondered. It was a city that, in 1938, had welcomed Hitler with wild parades and cheering crowds.

Vienna was of dual historic significance. In 1900, Jews had represented more than 10 percent of the population. Jewish luminaries such as Sigmund Freud, Albert Einstein, and Theodore Herzl (the founder of Zionism) had flourished, enlivening the coffeehouses with their impassioned intellectual exchanges.

But by the 1940s, the Jewish community had been all but extinguished. Many fled to the United States. Mostly all who stayed perished.

Whether or not it was universally true, Laura had been taught that Austrians were anti-Semitic. As some evidence of this, in 1986, they elected as their president Kurt Waldheim, a former Nazi collaborator. More recently, a younger neo Nazi had wielded power in the Austrian legislature through his extreme xenophobic right wing coalition.

In this context, they stepped foot on the turf of Austria, the nation that in World War II had been willingly annexed to Nazi Germany.

Two policemen stood on the platform, waiting for them with handcuffs.

"Byron, look."

"I know."

They should have stayed in Prague, where the citizens had a track record of resistance. More to the point, she should have resisted giving Byron a blow job on the train. What had she been thinking? Was she an exhibitionist? A masochist was more likely, if they were to land in jail.

The conductor signaled to the Viennese police. They approached, uttering German, and immediately fastened the handcuffs onto Laura and Byron.

"What are we going to do?" she cried.

Byron shrugged sheepishly. It was not the response Laura wanted.

"What are they saying?"

"That we are being arrested for lewd conduct in a public place."

They were dragged off the platform. Laura expected to be hauled off in a black SUV. Boxy vehicles—reminiscent of the ones the Nazis drove in WWII—were all the rage in the United States. But the officers brought them to a matchbox sized Volkswagen. Its white exterior was emblazoned with big block letters, POLIZEI.

Not long ago, an Illinois state trooper had pulled her over for driving eighty miles an hour on I-290. Laura's heart had thumped in her chest when the high beams flashed in her rearview mirror. As she'd handed over her license, registration, and insurance, her hands were shaking.

Now, Laura nearly laughed at the thought of this dwarf-like vehicle running down traffic violators let alone hardened criminals. Maybe she was at the core an outlaw!

Laura and Byron got into the back seat of the Volkswagen. *Le petite auto,* thought Laura in French, the wrong language for her circumstances. The sun was beating down on them. The navy blue interior was kept icy cold by the air conditioning. It was on full volume. The policemen—who both had pale blue eyes and nearly white blonde hair, sheared close to their scalps—got in the front. One pecked the keys on his palm-sized computer while the other toyed with the navigation screen.

"I've never been arrested before," said Laura, wishing she could squeeze his hand.

"Neither have I. But if I had to be arrested, I am glad that it is with you and for the charged offense," he said, managing a smile.

Laura shot him a contemptuous look.

"That did not come out right, did it?"

She shook her head no.

"I know your concern. I promise I will get us out of this jam."

She widened her eyes as if to say, "How?"

"I have friends in high places," he whispered.

Laura thought this sounded silly, but asked, "Who?"

He shushed her. He was not going to say and he wanted her

to stay quiet. If his hands were free, he could put a ball gag in her mouth. What had made her think of that? Possibly, it was these handcuffs, the basic beginner implements of kinky sex.

At home, she would have been able to call her father, who had his own friends in high places. Would she get one phone call in Austria? Had they been read their rights? If they had, they would have been in German, gibberish to her. In America, individuals had inalienable rights: Life, Liberty and the Pursuit of . . . Happiness. That was what Laura had been taught in grade school anyway. In the post—9/11 world, she was not so sure.

Suppose the Austrians did allow her to call her father. What would she say to him? "Hi, Dad. I'm being detained in Vienna for lewd conduct in a public place . . . No, you don't know him. We just met. And guess what? You're not going to believe this. *His* dad used to be a Nazi."

Her father had never forgiven the Germans. He refused to buy their cars and vowed never to enter their country.

The *Polizei*-mobile afforded minimal legroom. As they zoomed to the *Innerstadt* (Inner Ring) of the city, Laura's bare left knee knocked against Byron's right pant leg. They reached the police station. It was directly across the street from a charming café, the *Gefängnis*. Laura admired the striped awning and outdoor tables.

Byron noted, "It is named for its location. It means prison."

Polizei HQ, less menacing than Gestapo Central, had interior walls the color of green tea ice cream. It was clear to Laura that this was an institution and not some Imperial palace. She panicked when the policemen ordered them to go in opposite directions.

An attractive policewoman took her into custody. They proceeded through a set of thick metal doors.

The female officer was wearing a gray pencil skirt and matching tailored jacket. Her platinum hair was done up in a French twist. Laura thought she was very chic. She stood behind a high counter, asking Laura questions in heavily accented English and filling out forms. At the end of the countertop rested a gleaming black helmet, with a sharp spike rising from its center. It reminded Laura of the headgear worn by Hitler's henchmen.

The officer put down her pen. "We have new uniforms. There has been great controversy over the hats."

"I can see why. Your suit is nice."

"Thank you. I am not mussing up my hair with that thing." She derisively pointed to the helmet.

Smiling kindly, she held open the door to one of the jail cells and Laura obediently went inside. She was disappointed when the policewoman walked away, leaving her with her two cellmates.

She gingerly sat on a soiled cushion, ready to take in the grim reality of her situation. But immediately, as her buttocks touched down on the bench, she felt a wet squish-squish between her legs, in her crevice. She was still soaked from that episode on the train.

Or could it also be Byron's semen? She realized that he had come twice today—this morning under the Charles Bridge and this afternoon on the Euro Rail—and she had not come at all. The score thus far was 2-0, but should she be counting? They might be held in prison overnight, or worse, for several days, possibly weeks. She had no idea. Equaling the orgasm tally should be the least of her worries.

She studied her two cellmates. What were their crimes? Drugs? Prostitution? Having nowhere else to go?

An emaciated girl with black hair and dark skin was on a cot against the wall. She was curled in a fetal position and stared at Laura with blank black pupils. Her jeans were loose and she wore a red, ribbed tank top. She seemed so young. It was hard to determine her age. Her breasts may have stopped developing due to malnutrition.

The other cell occupant struck Laura as a crazy and younger version of herself. She too had long, straggly blonde hair. Her green eyes were glazed over and hollow. She started yelling at Laura in German, although the sounds were more like Icelandic yodeling.

Laura thought she might be a junkie or a deranged urchin. How long would it be before people thought similarly of her? Perhaps they already did.

And, with good reason. Laura admonished herself. Here she was, locked behind bars for blowing her boyfriend . . . openly and in broad daylight. Her two cellmates may be the unknowing byproducts of a cruel society. Laura, on the other hand, had cashed in on the accrued wealth of her stock options in order to finance this adventure. Some adventure. She argued with herself that she was in control.

Or was she? Was she that much different from the junkie and the whore? (Again, Laura chided herself, this time for having arrogantly tagged her cellmates.) She had discovered a potent drug. Its name was Lord Byron and it was *More, Now, Again*, to quote the title of the memoir of addiction by Elizabeth Wurtzel. She could never get enough.

The stylish female cop returned to the jail cell. "Congratulations, Laura. You are being released. Your stay with us was quite short. I hope you don't mind."

"Not at all." Laura breathed a huge sigh of relief. She glanced over her shoulder at the two others. The blonde street waif had stopped yodeling. The anorexic girl was gazing up at her like a scared kitten. Laura was free to go, but worried about the fates of her cellmates. "Are they going to be okay?"

"What do you think? At least in here they are safe."

"I suppose so."

"The small dark one was beaten and the other one self mutilates."

"Yin and yang."

A wave of powerlessness washed over Laura. For all her misgivings about being in a Germanic associated country, she was escaping unharmed. Ironically, she felt besieged on behalf of the two lost souls she was leaving behind. If only she could do something to help them.

As she was walking through the exit, two fists abruptly heaved against her back. Laura spun around. It was her younger blonde nemesis. Her hitherto dreamy eyes were now bulging spheres. Her fleshy mouth was wide open and she was screaming. In one swift movement, the trained officer shoved the madwoman into the cell and yanked Laura out. In the next instant, she locked the gate.

"There, there. She is a little jealous."

She handed Laura her pink backpack, which contained all of her belongings for the next few days. Byron was waiting for her outside, in front of the police station, with his black backpack slung over one shoulder. He seemed to Laura simultaneously both familiar and unfamiliar. When their eyes met, she felt as if she had known him her entire life. Love welled up inside of her. Yet Laura had to ask herself, who is this person? In truth, she hardly knew him, in spite of their sexual encounters.

*

She looks so beautiful, thought Byron as Laura approached him. "How are you?"

"I'm a little shaken," she replied.

"That is completely understandable. I am very sorry for this mess."

"A girl attacked me as I was leaving the jail cell."

What?! Byron felt his stomach drop. "Laura! Are you okay?"

"Yes. I'm fine."

"What happened? Who was she?"

"She punched me on my back. I think she was trying to push me out of the way so that she could get out of jail."

"Are you hurt?"

"I'm lucky. I'm out here and she's in there. How did you manage to get us released so quickly?"

"Are you sure you're not bruised? Perhaps I should examine you."

"Yes, you would like that, wouldn't you? Tell me. How did we get out?"

When Byron had first picked up the phone, he had believed that what he was about to do was their best option. It would be a surefire way to get the charges immediately dropped. He had not wanted Laura to spend any more time in jail.

"Please don't be upset with me," he said.

"Why would I be upset? I'm glad we're out. I'm relieved."

"I used my father's influence."

"What kind of influence does he have in Austria?"

"He knows someone in the government."

"It's not the neo Nazi guy is it? I forgot his name."

"Unfortunately, it is." He added, "He is no longer a neo Nazi. He is now a centrist. I suppose he finds this more advantageous than operating from the lunatic fringe."

"How well do you know him? Are you friends?"

"We have never met. My father knows his father. What can I say? A few phone calls and we are free."

"I must tell you, Byron, I feel kind of sick."

He did, too. "I'm sorry, Laura."

"We're free because of our connections with Nazis."

It was unseemly, Byron agreed. But he would not have allowed Laura to undergo legal interrogations about a blow job. That would have been needlessly humiliating and his fault.

He was about to defend his decision when Laura asked, "When you were growing up, Byron, what did your father teach you?"

Byron knew where this question was going. It was reasonable for her to want to establish—beyond a shadow of a doubt—that he held no anti-Semitic views.

He answered honestly and smiled at the memory. "He taught me how to play your American game of baseball. For my fifth birthday, he gave me my first baseball bat, ball, and glove."

"Really? Where did he learn to play in Germany?"

"He researched it. He was fascinated with the poetry of baseball. It is replete with metaphors, after all. Stealing bases, striking out, hitting a home run—"

"You're good at that."

"You think so? In what way?"

"When I was young, getting to first base meant kissing. Second base was letting the boy feel your breasts. Going to third was touching down *there*. Reaching home plate was—"

"You and I?" Byron teased.

"Also known as a 'grand slam'!"

"I like that." He was glad that Laura had taken on a playful tone. "But we digress. What else did your father teach you?"

"He taught me about the romantic poets and their idealization of women and love. We never discussed Jewish girls. They were not part of the lesson plan."

"Why would they be? Were there any Jewish girls in post-war Germany?"

"You're right. I'm sorry."

"It's just the way it was. It wasn't your fault."

That much was true. Byron had been born more than a decade after the war had ended. There was something else that he wanted to share with her. It was his long held secret. "Their absence may be why Jewish girls held such a powerful mystique for me. When I was a teenager, I fantasized about being with one of them."

"Which one?"

"I didn't know any. You."

"Wow. Really?"

"Yes. Exactly you," Byron said.

"Maybe you were subconsciously rebelling against your father's Nazi past. Maybe you still are."

"It is possible, but it is much, much more than that, Laura."

CHAPTER 8:
JUDENPLATZ

"Where do we go from here?" Laura asked. They were stopped at a crosswalk at a busy intersection. The police station was located in a commercial district and the area was congested with rush hour traffic.

"It's early," Byron said, despite it being the late afternoon. "Vienna was not on our original itinerary, but now that we're here, would you like to see some of the city before getting back on the train?"

"I would like to see something other than the jail."

"So would I." The light changed and they crossed, holding hands. They went down one of the side streets. It was under a canopy of trees and aligned a park. Young boys were playing—of all things—baseball. Laura and Byron continued past the field. They proceeded up a wide set of stairs that took them to a church. From there, they wandered through a cobbled passage. At the end was the entrance to a courtyard. Medieval letters etched into the walls spelled out the word, "*Judenplatz.*"

"This was the Jewish Square," Byron said. They went in.

In the center of the courtyard, there stood a white concrete monolith. Laura and Byron approached it, again holding hands.

The names of concentration camps were engraved in all four sides. It was a memorial to the Holocaust. Tourists wearing black tank tops and running shoes lounged against it.

He guided her past the slouching sightseers. Laura gazed down at the numerous inscriptions: Dachau, Bergen-Belsen, Auschwitz, Birkenau, Riga, Theresienstadt, Sachsenhausen, Buchenwald, Treblinka, and still others. Byron—in a sincere display of empathy— squeezed her hand. It was too much, considering his Nazi background. Tears welled up in her eyes. Laura thought, whatever he does, he manages to make me wet in some part of my body.

She felt guilty for thinking about sex in such a solemn setting. Blackbirds fluttered and squalled about them. She was aware of their ominous hue and throaty mating calls. A soldier was several yards away. He was wearing camouflage fatigues and had weaponry strapped to his body. Laura let go of Byron's hand and walked toward the armed guard.

"What are you protecting?"

"*Das museum.*" He pointed his rifle upward at the Museum *Judenplatz.*

Byron and Laura agreed to check it out.

The Museum *Judenplatz* contained the archeological remains of a synagogue, burned to the ground by the pogroms in 1421. While preparing the area for redevelopment in the late twentieth century, excavators had uncovered the vestiges. The building plans were scrapped and a museum showcasing the temple remnants was opened instead.

It was near closing time. They advanced through a tube that was theatrically lit, climbed shallow steps, and entered a large exhibition space. The room was painted black. Spotlights illuminated white stalagmite slabs.

A crystalline block in the center of the room was labeled "*Bimah.*" Another opalescent mass was named "Torah Ark." The place markers identified what one was looking at. There were no actual Torah scrolls or other religious objects. Laura was curious about a sign at the far edge of the room that read "*Frauenshul.*"

From the two German words, "*frau*" and "*shul,*" Laura knew that "*frauenschul*" meant "women's synagogue." Laura went over to inspect it. In the Middle Ages—as well as in twenty-first century Orthodox synagogues—women were not allowed to worship with the men.

A draft of freezing air enveloped her. Byron stroked the skin on the back of her neck. He lifted up all of her long hair, sending quivers down her spine. She now understood the dangers of men and women sitting next to one another in a *shul.* It was much too distracting. How could one concentrate on prayers? Except for ones that involved men?

He released her hair. It spilled across her shoulders. She glanced down. Unlike the rest of the floor, which was gleaming granite, the ground on which they stood—the foundation of the *frauenschul*—was brown clay. Laura thought it suitable for a sexual take-down.

Byron tilted her face and passionately kissed her on the mouth. Her lips tingled from his touch. Against the thin cloth of her dress, she could feel his rod pressing against her mound. She felt a surge and knew she was wet. When would it stop? Would she ever get enough?

"Should we be doing this in public? Again?"

"You're right," he admitted. A fence ran along the perimeter of the room. It was composed of the same jagged quartz substance. They went behind it. Byron got down on his knees. He stroked and planted kisses on her calves.

"Your skin is so soft," he said. He wasted no time in moving his hands up her legs and beneath her short dress. Laura pretended to be in the fifteenth century, clothed completely in a virgin wool garment. She was filled with forbidden desire in a holy place for a *man*. The only question was: Who was *this* man? Who was Byron? Was he a young and sexy Torah scholar or one of the ravagers of the pogrom?

Had he adequately answered her earlier questions about how he really felt about Jews? Was he an ally or the enemy?

He reached for her panties and yanked them off with one skilled motion. Laura stepped out of them. Byron stood up, removed his trousers, and pulled her toward him. "Are you ready for me, *Geliebte*?"

"*Geliebte*? What is that?"

"A German word for lover. But not in the casual sense. It implies a deeply emotional and physical connection. I feel that we belong together. Don't you, Laura?"

"Yes, I do!" Her body grew hot in response to their mutual declaration.

He stuck two fingers in her heart-shaped, dripping locket. It immediately evoked for Laura the image of Dali's meltingly distorted clock. Time was running out. The museum would soon be closed. Byron held Laura against the temple wall relic.

He grabbed her ass, lifted her up, and pushed Lord Byron inside of her. He moved in rapid thrusts. The pointy surface of the wall was jabbing her in the back. She was being stabbed from within and without. She gasped and cried out. Byron covered her mouth to stifle her screams. With one final climactic shove, he moaned uncontrollably.

He held her in place. They heard the sudden click-clack of footsteps. Static from a two-way radio echoed nearby.

"No, no, not again," whispered Laura. If they were arrested for a second time in twenty-four hours for the same offense of lewd behavior in a public place, surely the Austrian authorities would toss them back in jail and throw away the keys.

He released her from his grasp. Lord Byron slid out of her, smearing Laura's legs with his milk and her honey. Byron quickly zipped up his pants. Despite the weakness in her knees, Laura rushed to the exit without him.

He called after her, holding up her panties, and said, "*Geliebte*, aren't you forgetting these?"

CHAPTER 9:
SERGEI

Laura and Byron caught the last train of the day from Vienna to Bratislava. The trip lasting less than an hour was chaste for the two of them. A pizza-shaped moon rose over the landscape of Slovakia.

In Bratislava, they grabbed a cab for the ride to the artist's loft. The driver deposited them in front of a distressed building that was punctured with holes.

"Bullet holes," remarked Byron.

"From World War II?"

"Yes and from before. You see this quite often in Eastern Europe."

Plastic sheets—rather than glass panes—covered blown out windows of the building. They rippled in the nighttime breeze. Hadn't the war ended in the prior millennium?

Sergei, the artist, greeted them at the front door on the ground level. "Please excuse the condition of this place. There was a camera crew here today. They're shooting a film about the end of the world."

The three of them marched up the stairs to Sergei's loft, which was on the third floor. The door was open and Sergei gestured grandly for Laura to enter before the men.

"Welcome to my loft. Welcome to Bratislava."

Intense track lighting overwhelmed her. Tawdry translucent sculptures lined the circumference of the room and were illuminated from within.

Sergei ran his fingers through a thicket of shiny black hair. Laura wondered what brand of cheap Eastern European hair gel he used. Yet she noted the expert haircut, as if he had just stepped out of a posh salon on Chicago's Magnificent Mile.

Laura could not take her eyes off him. A white t-shirt was a mere film loosely covering his thin torso. Its short sleeves scarcely capped his shoulders. Sergei's scrawny arms were unexpectedly defined by bulging biceps.

As he smiled at her, Sergei displayed a set of ideally squared and blindingly white teeth. Laura smiled back. Had Sergei been to an orthodontist? Had he had his teeth bleached? Who was this guy? Was he a starving artist or a trust fund poseur playing that part?

According to Byron, Sergei had escaped from Soviet-controlled East Germany by vaulting over the Berlin Wall as a young boy. He must have been an infant or embryonic, thought Laura. It had been two decades since the Communists had ruled.

"Feel free to look around." Sergei glanced at his watch. "I'm going to get ready to go out."

Byron and Laura circled the loft, holding hands. This was a comfort to Laura as she realized she was feeling weak. Sergei's sculptures were icons from the Cold War, decorated to resemble cartoon characters.

Joseph Stalin was portrayed as Superman. The letter S was emblazoned on his chest. Under Stalin, the Soviets had liberated Auschwitz. This "Superman" had also conducted the Great Purge, executing or exiling to Siberia millions of people. Laura tried to perceive the irony. What was the intention of the artist?

Mikhail Gorbachev was evidently Spider-Man. A net replaced that sprawling Rorschach-like birthmark on his forehead. Ronald Reagan was a cowboy riding roughshod on a carousel horse. It was clever. It was kitsch. Was it art?

Byron let go of her hand and stepped back from the sculptures. "I see an infatuation with the vulgarity and freedom of Western culture at odds with the longing for the parental protection of the Old Regime."

Sergei and Laura looked at Byron confusedly.

"Actually, I—" Sergei began and then dismissed his response to Byron's analysis. "I have plenty of time to hang out with you. The

Underground doesn't open until one a.m."

What kind of topsy-turvy city was this? "One a.m.? In Chicago, that is when our trains *stop* running," Laura said.

"Silly girl. There are no subways in Bratislava. The Underground is a disco." Sergei went on to explain that the club was in a former bomb shelter, burrowed in a hill beneath the Bratislava Castle. "Would you like to come along?"

He was looking dead on at Laura.

His slanted black eyes, reminiscent of the Mongolians of the Far East, mesmerized her. She was further attracted to his pushed in Slavic nose. For a not-so-fleeting moment, she thought of kissing his full burgundy lips.

"We'll stay here," Byron said. "We're rather tired. Isn't that right, Laura?"

"Right," she concurred. She was feeling dizzy. Aside from Byron's semen, she had eaten very little all day. "Byron, I'm hungry."

"I wish I had some food to offer you," said Sergei. "I am a lousy cook and there is no stove here anyway. I do have vodka. Would you like some?"

"No, thank you."

She stood in the center of the loft. She had had dizzy spells before. They had occurred at work and were likely due to job stress. There she could grab onto her desk until the vertigo passed. Sergei's loft was one open vastness with no supporting columns to grab.

She began to panic. The closest thing to a pillar was Sergei. Laura tumbled toward him and into his arms. She immediately smelled his pungent body odor. It revived her like smelling salts. At about six feet tall, he loomed over her. Was that a hard on in his jeans? She could feel his shaft hitting her belly button. He held her steady by pinching her arms.

"Are you okay, Laura?" Byron asked. He had been her lover, officially, for all of six hours.

"I'm fine now," she said.

"Are you sure?"

"Yes." She straightened up. Sergei guided her to the wall and a chair, in which she collapsed.

"I'll run downstairs and find something for you to eat," said Byron. To Sergei he said, "Is there any place open in your neighborhood?"

"The restaurants in Bratislava generally stop serving at ten. Fortunately, there's a café on the next block that's an exception to this rule. Go out the front door and make a left. Make another left and start down the hill. Take your first right and you should see it."

Was he sending Byron on a wild goose chase?

Laura dreaded eating Slovakian food, especially if it had been sitting around all day. It could very well be wild goose, as gamey repasts were common in Bohemia. Or he might return with sausages, which she did not ever eat (except the male ones). She missed Chicago, where she could get a decent meal at any hour, night and day.

"I'll be right back," Byron said and bolted out the door.

She was sitting in a shocking pink canvas chair of the midcentury Mod style. It was low to the ground. Laura tilted back her head, stretched out her legs, and pretended she was at the beach.

Sergei tore off his t-shirt, revealing a patch of black hair in the center of his chest. "I won't go anywhere until you feel better. I'll stay right here. If you want me to," he added.

Were those traces of a surfer dude accent, à la Sean Penn in *Fast Times at Ridgemont High*? Seriously. What did Laura know about accents? She had been wrong before. She had been wrong about Byron.

Anyway, accents can be faked. Laura herself was confident that she could mimic the vocal inflections of Eastern European girls. She knew these young women to be outwardly bewildered and inwardly self-reliant. She was anxious to try out this seductive trick on unsuspecting Midwestern boys when she returned to the States. If she ever returned.

She suddenly became aware of herself as a forty-five-year-old woman in the presence of a much younger (twenty-five-year-old?) man. No doubt, the wrinkles under her eyes were visible in the stark lighting of the loft. It hardly mattered because at this moment, his gaze was fixed on those same naked calves Byron had caressed in the destroyed synagogue. Before coming here, she had not had sex in ten months. Now it seemed that there were two men who wanted to do her.

"Don't worry about me," she said. "If I stay still in this chair, I'll be okay."

"I guess I'll get ready."

Sergei went somewhere behind her. She listened to him take a piss and flush the toilet. A knob squeaked and then there was a loud gush of water. It drummed against what Laura visualized as a hollow, plastic, and portable shower stall.

More water gurgled in the antebellum pipes encased somewhere behind her head. Laura closed her eyes and said, "I am in Bratislava. Brat-is-lava, Brat-is-lava, Brat-is-lava." She had not even heard of this place until yesterday. Tears, not of sadness, but of exhaustion, ran down her cheeks.

Soon afterwards, Sergei emerged—damp and sporting a slinky black shirt unbuttoned to his naval—and bid her goodbye.

CHAPTER 10:
SUSPENDED IN SLOVAKIA

It was now 11 p.m. On the floor of Sergei's loft, Laura and Byron were eating cut up fruit and slices of cheese and drinking bottled water. He had also managed to find a baguette. Even in its hard, crunchy, stale state, the French bread was delicious. It whetted her appetite for more food. There wasn't much, but it would hold them over until morning. She felt her strength returning. She started to stand up to test her equilibrium.

Byron grabbed her wrists and forced her back down.

"Stay right where you are," he ordered. "You are my prisoner."

The son of a Nazi was holding her captive. Those horrific photos! They would not leave her head. They were of the victims, of piled up dead bodies and skeletal living beings. GIs had taken the photos on Eisenhower's command. The great American General had had the foresight to know that at some point in the future, Holocaust deniers would emerge.

"Tell me, Lady Laura, what are you thinking?"

"Nothing. I'm digesting my food," she said, feeling that this was an unladylike thing to say. "And us."

"What about us?"

"How you used a neo Nazi to get us out of jail. What does that make me? Whose side am I on?"

"My side," he said, pulling her up from the floor. "We share the same beliefs. Does using the influence of an Austrian right wing nut job make me morally despicable? I am not sure. What do you think?"

"I think . . . I did not . . . exactly turn myself around and go back to the jail."

He smiled. "That's my Laura."

"What about your father?"

"He is my father. He is not me."

They stood facing each other with their bodies touching. "I don't want any of this coming between us," he added.

"It is already between us. You confessed that you always wanted to be with a Jewish girl. I am that Jewish girl. You are attracted to me because of my religion. You want to inflict pain and torture on me as a means of identifying with your father."

"Now you are spouting psychobabble."

"I sound like you, Byron, when you are talking about art."

He laughed. "Come here." He pulled her even closer.

"What about the Hasidic book? You saw me reading it."

"I noticed *you* before I saw the book. Trust me. It was not the book that drew me to you."

"Why did you call me your prisoner?"

"I have—as I have had from the moment we met—an overwhelming urge to possess you." He kissed her deeply on the mouth. He let go of her wrists and went for her hair, which he pulled.

She was wet, for the umpteenth time in the past eighteen hours. He turned her on, irrespective of the whole Nazi thing.

There was no bed in the room. Instead, there was a hammock strung up near the street-facing windows. Was this where Sergei slept each night?

"Get in the hammock," Byron commanded.

Laura obeyed him. She gazed up at the rope and the ceiling hooks from which the hammock dangled. It swayed and creaked. It was like being on a dinghy in choppy waters.

"Let's see what toys Sergei keeps in his loft," said Byron. He inspected Sergei's cartoonish sculptures. The polyurethane figures were aglow, powered by electricity. Byron unplugged the cords and carried them back to Laura. He dropped them on the floor beside the hammock.

Byron tugged at the hem of her dress and helped her pull the garment over her head. It was a relief to be out of it! She had been living in this same floral frock since the morning. It had seen an illicit blow job, a jail cell, and sex in an ancient synagogue.

She had removed her bra and stuffed it in her backpack hours ago, sometime in Vienna. All she had on now were her panties. Byron told her to turn over.

She lie face down on the hammock. Byron tied each of four electrical cords to an unoccupied curtain rod. Tape held up the plastic sheets that served as window dressings. He slid off her panties. He tied one cable to each wrist. Then he forced apart her legs and tied one cable to each ankle. She was suspended. Laura reflected that in this flayed position, her body took on the shape of a swastika.

Byron removed his shirt and wrapped it around Laura's eyes, blindfolding her.

"Now what?"

"Keep quiet."

A key jangled. She heard a door open and the soft pattering of footsteps. She suspected the presence of another man in the room. It had to be Sergei. She remembered his scent, despite the recent shower. What would be his reaction to seeing her tied up like this?

Unidentified fingers encircled her mouth. She sucked on the fingers. They tasted bitter, evoking turpentine. This had to be the artist, Sergei. Laura thought fleetingly that she could be poisoning herself. Hadn't he just scrubbed himself clean? What had he *really* been doing in the shower? Thinking of her? Of doing this? Laura *wished.* The fumes could be embedded in his pores. Regrettably, the hand retreated.

"Please. Help me, someone. Who are you? I need you."

A plastic ball was stuffed in her mouth.

She heard a zipper unzip. The hammock below her squeaked as if accommodating the new weight of a body. As she was hanging face down, Laura felt the head of a cock tap upwards on her belly.

Then there were multiple hands cupping her breasts and squeezing her nipples. Instinctively, she started to scream in a combination of ecstasy and pain. Yet her cries were hushed by the ball in her mouth.

The introductory slap shocked her. She squealed into the gag. They smacked her repeatedly, alternating from one side of her ass to the other. The steady rhythm caused Laura to swing to and fro—in midair. To Laura, the movement was more disconcerting than the spanking. First, she easily got motion sickness. (What if she got so nauseous, she vomited into the gag and suffocated?) Second, if her short-term memory served her correctly, the plaster on these four walls was crumbling. She imagined the rod—to which the cables were secured—detaching from the wall. She began to panic. Was Byron acting out an unconscious desire to inflict upon her Nazi torture? With the window wide open, Byron and Sergei could easily hit this one (her!) right out of the park.

Mercifully, the spanking—and with it, the batting about—stopped. Someone traced his finger from her throat to the start of her V. Someone pushed back her hair, kissed her on the forehead, and moved away. She heard footsteps fade in the distance and a door close. Who had just left and who had stayed behind? Sergei had intrigued her, but she longed for Byron.

The man—whoever he was—loosened the cables and lovingly lowered her into the hammock. Her muscles ached from being stretched, contorted, and held in one place for so long. She relaxed in his arms as he gathered up her limp body and transported her across the loft. They floated together in the darkness. He gently released her, this time on a bumpy, unstable, and rolling surface. He took out the gag and untied the blindfold.

It was Byron. "I love you!" she exclaimed.

What did she say? Did she mean it? If this abandonment of control and unquenchable desire was love, then yes, she did mean it.

She waited for his response. Given the awkward situation, most guys would at least mutter "I love you, too" with their words all running together and at an almost inaudible decibel level. Not so, her Byron. It felt like an eternity before his lips parted. And even then, he said nothing.

He kissed her on the mouth and on her face. She was disappointed, but tried to be reasonable about it. They had basically just met. She looked around her and saw where they were, in a crate of plastic balls, like the ones they have at a McDonald's Play Land. Only in Bratislava, thought Laura. At long last, Byron put his fingers into her hole and attentively, fervently touched her. It was seconds before she came. She erupted recklessly, as the McDonald's balls spun and gave way under her and she heard Byron say, "I love you, I love you, I love you, too."

CHAPTER 11:
SEXBOMBE

She woke up after a long, deep, and restful sleep. The previous day had been one of the most eventful of her entire life. To her surprise, Byron was not at her side. Where was he? She looked out across the loft. His black leather backpack was on the floor, in the exact spot where he had left it the night before. Laura was tempted to unzip the backpack and go through Byron's personal effects, but quickly ignored this impulse. She climbed out of the McDonald's crate of plastic balls.

She went to her own backpack and checked her cell phone to find out what time it was. It was after one in the afternoon! She must have been really tired. She called out in the quietness of the loft, "Byron? Sergei? Is anyone here?"

I guess not, thought Laura, as no one answered. She decided to take a shower.

The shower stall was as Laura had imagined it the night before. It barely contained her frame and she was quite small! How did Sergei manage to squeeze in here? It rocked in response to her every movement. She thoroughly scrubbed her body and vigorously washed her hair. Who knew what she could have picked up in the Viennese jail cell? The place had seemed immaculate, in perhaps typical German/ Austrian meticulousness, which was reassuring to Laura.

She then brushed her teeth three times, running the water and spitting into a deep metal sink. Flat tools were on the ledge, along with a tin of turpentine. Ah-hah! Could this be the evidence that Sergei was in the room with them the night before? Laura unscrewed the cap and sniffed. She recalled the taste of turpentine on Sergei's fingertips in her mouth. It would be toxic to do an actual taste test and drink from the canteen.

Laura had packed two changes of clothes, Capri jeans to wear during the day and a coquettish dress for going out at night.

She chose the little black dress that was intended for evening. She pinned up her long blonde hair, allowing some of the locks to fall on her face and down her back. Eyeing a set of baubles on one of Sergei's sculptures—Margaret Thatcher done up as Minnie Mouse—Laura decided that she could use some jewelry. Why not? She removed the necklace and put it on. The strand was so long that it reached down to her knees. She doubled it up. As she walked to leave the loft, she could feel the bubble beads tapping against her mound. *The center of my being*, thought Laura. *Perfect.*

She emerged from Sergei's building. The sun blinded her eyes and she put on her vintage 60s shades. They had been a last-minute purchase in the States before leaving for Prague.

Her shocking pink and lime green sneakers notwithstanding, she was dressed from head to toe like a movie star. *Who is that girl?* Laura thought. She stood at the top of a rickety hill. There was no way she would have been able to negotiate this incline in heels.

Something suddenly possessed her. Yesterday, *two* men had wanted her. Last night, *two* men had teased, tormented, and desired her. Contrast this to her former self as a workaholic, whose sexuality had all but disappeared. As she gazed down on the houses of this anonymous street, she felt that she was the First Brat of Bratislava. Better still, the Empress of Eastern Europe!

She proceeded down the hill and walked a few more blocks until she reached the Danube River. Taking in its glimmering expanse, she was reminded of Lake Michigan. She decided that this corner of the earth was her new hometown.

A monstrosity of a bridge soared above the river. At the foot of the overpass was a plaque. It commemorated the site of what had been the Jewish Quarter of Bratislava. The Soviet government had demolished it when rebuilding the city. Any traces of a Slovak

Jewry had been vaporized.

Wherever Laura went in her newly conquered Empire, she was confronted with the tragic plight of the Jews. This had never been the case in America. She was growing weary and immune to the Jews' suffering.

Maybe she was on Jew overload. Laura knew that tourists in Florence, from viewing so many art masterpieces, complained of wooziness in the museums. Enough Da Vinci, Raphael, and Michelangelo! Enough flawless renderings of the Pietà, the Virgin Mary cradling a deceased Christ! Give me a Grant Wood painting of a man and a woman with a pitchfork any day!

Worse, could this be what happens when a Jewish female hooks up with a German male? Laura tried to push this premise out of her mind.

The imposing Bratislava Castle loomed nearby. Laura was not interested in doing any more sightseeing for now. She opened her guidebook to the map of Bratislava. From where she stood, all winding roads led to the Old Town. She wanted to grab some breakfast (at two p.m.).

It was a short walk to the Old Town where the atmosphere was quite lively. At one of the many outdoor cafés, Laura found an empty table. It was adjacent to six gorgeous young men. They seemed to be conversing in Italian. One of the guys wore a red soccer shirt with matching shorts over an impressive bulge. His legs were deeply tanned. He winked at Laura. There. It was happening again.

Byron appeared out of nowhere. He kissed her the European way, on both cheeks.

"Good morning. Or should I say, good afternoon, *Geliebte*."

"I was looking for you."

"You have found me," he said joyfully. "We have found each other."

"Where did you go?"

"I went out to get you a gift." He was holding a shopping bag. "You were sleeping so soundly. I did not want to wake you."

"Can I see it?"

"When the time is right. It is a surprise."

Just then, Sergei showed up, wearing faded cutoffs. He wedged himself between Laura and Byron. He scraped the metal chair across the cobbled ground. Laura thought that his pale legs were the color of a Siberian winter. The black hairs on his calves were the soot gusting over all of Russia from Moscow to the Far East hinterlands.

"You look ravishing this morning," he said to her.

"She is my *sexbombe*," Byron said.

"Huh, bro?" said Sergei.

"Don't you speak German?"

"No. I speak Russian, English, and a little Polish."

"It is the German word for sexpot."

"Even I knew that," Laura said.

"You look like Brigitte Bardot," Sergei said. They all laughed.

"Thank you," said Laura. "Did you ever see the film by Jean-Luc Godard, *Contempt*?"

Byron replied yes. Sergei replied no.

"It stars Brigitte Bardot. Throughout most of the movie, she keeps saying to her husband, 'I have contempt for you. I have contempt for you.' She says it over and over again. She says it in French, of course."

"Say it in French."

"*J'ai le mepris pour toi*." Laura spoke in her perfect schoolgirl French.

"Why does she have contempt for him?" asked Byron.

"He tries to fix her up with another man."

"Hah! That!" Sergei slapped his knee. "That's no big deal."

"Do you have contempt for me, Laura?"

"No. I do not have contempt for you, Byron."

"What about for me?"

"Nor do I have contempt for you, Sergei. In fact, I have no

contempt for any man on this planet today."

"Today is a glorious day. We must celebrate." Byron signaled to the waiter that they were ready to order. The waiter soon returned with a tray of gritty coffee, small chocolate cakes, and glasses of flat warm water.

"Sergei, here are the papers for you to sign."

"What are those?" Laura asked.

"I am going to be Sergei's exclusive art dealer."

"Your Byron is quite the salesman."

"There are buyers in Berlin. We are going there next," Byron told her.

"We are?"

"Yes. You and I."

"I have never been to Germany."

"You can visit the bunker where Hitler and Eva Braun hid out and committed suicide. Byron told me that you are Jewish," remarked Sergei.

"Yes, I am," she said, not sure what—if anything—he was implying. Her mind went quickly to another subject. "I didn't bring enough clothes. I won't have anything to wear in Germany."

The men laughed. They both said, "You don't need clothes when you are with—"

"Us," said Sergei.

"Me," said Byron.

Sergei signed the papers and placed the pen on the glass tabletop with a ceremonious thud.

They raised and clanked their water glasses. Laura drank up. She was thirsty.

Byron said, "When we are in Berlin, I will introduce you to my father."

The water came gushing out of her mouth. "Your father?"

"*Oy vey*," added Sergei. "There's a bomb for y'all."

Who was this guy? He was an amalgam of many cultures, but

with no traces of his purported country of origin, East Germany.

"*Oy vey* is right," Laura agreed. "There is no way I can meet your father."

"I want you to meet him. I want to show you off."

"Are you going to tell him that I am Jewish?"

"I'm not sure. We'll see how it goes." He displayed a pair of airline tickets in paper Lufthansa jackets. "Tomorrow, we fly to Berlin."

CHAPTER 12:
THE RAZOR'S EDGE

She was down to her last outfit, Capri jeans with a camisole under a cropped blazer, which she now hugged to her chest. They were standing curbside at the Berlin airport, waiting for a cab. They had traveled north and the change in climate was startling. The sky was dark gray and it was drizzling. There was a chill in the air. Laura contemplated digging in her backpack for the black trench coat that was scrunched at the bottom. Before she could, a taxi screeched to a halt in front of them. They got inside.

In German, Byron told the driver the name and location of the hotel. The car raced through a neighborhood at the edge of Berlin that Byron explained was Turkish. Did the cab driver think they were on the Autobahn? He was driving that fast and crazily. After several hairpin turns, they landed on a fashionable boulevard. They skidded on to a semicircular driveway.

Two doormen bedecked in uniforms with tassels rushed to the cab. They opened the car doors with their white-gloved hands. Laura leaped out, while Byron paid the fare. Lamps from overhead warmed the red-carpeted entrance.

They entered the opulent hotel lobby. Laura identified the décor as "faux Old World," meaning that the furnishings had the grandeur of a bygone era, but were decidedly brand new.

Crystal chandeliers hung from the ceiling. The mirrors, the Corinthian columns, and even the planters were trimmed with gold. The previous evening, they had slept twisted together in Sergei's hammock. The night before that was spent in a box of hard, plastic balls. Three days ago, they had made their bed on the mushy ground beneath the Charles Bridge. Laura was willing to put her

Bohemian adventure on hold for a day or two, in favor of *this*.

Their hotel room smelled of lilacs. A fluffy white duvet covered an immense bed with oversized pillows. They had never before made love in such luxury, or on a mattress supported by boxed springs, for that matter. She was eager to try out the new setup.

"Laura, come here." Byron called to her from the bathroom.

"Wow," was all she could say. The floor, walls, and ceiling were tiled with marble. Thick white towels were neatly folded and stacked on shelves. The toilet was discretely hidden in a closet. Set aside from the glassed-in shower and the dressing area was an oval tub. It boasted a dozen spigots.

"Let's check out the German plumbing, shall we? It is the most technologically advanced in the world, as one might expect. Watch this." Byron turned on the main faucet. The basin immediately filled up with hot water and blue bubbles. Steam rose from the surface.

Laura was in awe.

"I will be right back," he said. "Feel free to take off all of your clothes."

"Where are you going?"

"Nowhere. I need to get something from my bag."

Laura removed her clothes and stepped out of her shoes. The marble floor was heated. She dipped her toes in the water. It was scorching! Like my desire for Byron, Laura thought. When you play with fire, must you always get burned?

She added cold water and waited for it to lower the overall temperature of the pool. Once it did, she got in. She squeezed liquid soap onto a sea sponge and washed her face and hair and body.

Byron returned. He was carrying a razor blade and a can of shaving cream. Laura agreed that he needed a shave. They were going to meet his father later on for dinner.

He spurted the foam onto his open palm. It reminded Laura of whipped cream on a hot fudge sundae.

"Stand up," he said.

Although she had just gotten in, Laura stood up in the tub,

doing as she was told. Her body was dripping. The air on her skin was cool. Her blonde hair was darkened and stringy from the water and hung over her nipples. He smacked the pile of shaving cream on her pubic mound.

"What are you doing?"

"Have you been shaved before?"

"No."

"Do you want me to?"

"Well . . . why not? There is a first time for everything." She said this more bravely than she felt. As he shaved her, catching the short curlicues and milky gobbets in his free hand, a horrifying image flashed through Laura's mind: A Nazi was shearing the head of a gaunt Jewish woman. This had been common practice in the camps.

"How are you doing?" he asked.

"Fine," she lied.

"Open your legs now." The razor was dangerously close to the folds of her inner labia. If anything, her own risky predicament distracted Laura from further thoughts of the Holocaust.

After he finished shaving her, he left her alone, still standing in the tub, and went to one of the sinks to rinse off his hands. He came back with a cool damp cloth and very carefully wiped her clean.

Then he took off all of his clothes and joined her in the jetted tub. Together, they sat down in the swirling tides of water.

He grabbed her damp head and kissed her passionately. They submerged deeply. The suds came up to their chins. One of his hands wrapped around her neck while the other reached for her dome. With his thumb, he touched her newly virgin skin. He pushed another finger into her hole. Laura gasped. As he plunged his tongue into her mouth, Laura knew that there was nothing between them now—nothing.

CHAPTER 13:
JOSEF SPEAKS

He presented her with a bubblegum pink sequined tube dress. Laura was able to step into it and pull it up over her torso and breasts. The dress had no sleeves or shoulder straps. It fit her like a skin-tight glove. There was more: He reached into the shopping bag and pulled out a pair of black patent leather lace-up stiletto sandals.

The outfit was the mystery gift Byron had purchased for her in Bratislava.

She slipped on the flimsy shoes and tied their thin plastic cords just above her ankles. For an instant, she was reminded of the time he had tied her up with electrical cables in Bratislava.

"This is a really nice outfit." It was an understatement. "Thank you so much."

"My pleasure," he murmured.

"How did you know my sizes?"

"I checked your clothes and shoes sizes while you were sleeping that first morning in Bratislava."

"I love it," Laura gushed. "Although I'm not sure that this is the appropriate thing for me to be wearing when I meet your father."

"I'm not sure, either," Byron admitted. "I want you to wear it anyway."

"Are you going to tell him that I am Jewish?"

"I already have."

"Oh." She was suddenly overcome with modesty. She remembered her lightweight black trench coat, stuffed at the bottom of her backpack. Just before leaving their room, Laura grabbed it and put it on. It was wrinkled, damp, and smelled of the polluted rains of Eastern Europe.

"You're wearing that?"

"It's cold in Berlin."

"We'll be inside. We're meeting my father in the hotel restaurant."

"I know. Just a little self-conscious. . ."

"Don't be. Let's not cover up the pretty party dress I bought for the occasion."

Interesting choice, she thought. He helped her remove the coat. She carried it across her arm as they went out the door.

The cavernous dining room was filled with posh people and the din of their conversations. One humongous chandelier, seemingly weighted down by its crystal ornaments, illuminated the room.

Laura imagined the chandelier swinging perilously and crashing to the floor as the Allies bombed Berlin during Hitler's final days. She pictured Eva Braun in a red flapper dress, dancing on a tabletop, as the walls caved in all around her. She thought of Eva with a shotgun in her mouth, blowing out her brains.

The ultimate blow job, Laura shuddered, wondering if she had anything in common with the Third Reich's It Girl. Was Laura likewise in denial?

In the corner of the room, at a round table for four, a man sat alone. Although she had never seen a photograph of him, Laura somehow knew that the solidly built man with a full head of silver hair was Byron's father.

Sure enough, it was. "Papa," Byron called out, fetching Laura by the hand and dragging her across the room. He sounded like a young boy when he said this, but then Laura remembered that Papa was German for Dad.

They vigorously shook both hands and hugged. If Byron harbored any untoward feelings regarding his father, they were all but absent. A halo of love seemed to encircle them.

Byron introduced his father to Laura as Mr. Baumgaarten.

"Please. Call me Josef."

Laura thought of Josef as a Jewish name, but remembered that it was also the first name of Goebbels, Hitler's right hand man and chief propagandist. The Karl Rove of his day, Laura thought wryly.

Josef stared at Laura. He looked her up and down and then nodded approvingly at his son. He was, how old? She thought eighty, or was he eighteen? For all he had witnessed as a youth, he still seemed rather sprightly and carefree. Wasn't he the teeniest besieged with guilt?

The three of them sat down. It was the first time Laura had tried sitting in the constricting tube dress. She feared it was creating the illusion of more cleavage than she actually possessed and for Josef's view. It was also rubbing against the area that Byron had just shaved. She felt sweat dripping from her armpits.

The two men spoke to one another in German. Laura suspected that they were talking about her.

So this is who he is, thought Laura. His Swiss boarding school-inspired accent might be cute, but he is downright sexy when speaking in his native tongue. She felt that she was glimpsing his essence. Why was he single? Surely, any German-speaking woman with whom he conversed would find him irresistible.

The older man speaking in German had a different effect on Laura. The guttural sounds coming from Josef made her think of Nazis.

A busboy interrupted the discussion. He filled their glasses with water, sloppily spilling some of it on Laura's legs. As he departed, Josef rolled his eyes. He smiled at Laura and held out his napkin. While she had her own, she accepted his. "Thank you."

Laura dried her legs and Mr. Baumgaarten said, "Byron tells me you are Jewish. Did any of your relatives perish in the war?"

He certainly took no time getting to the point. In this way, he was like his son. "No. My family went to America long before that, before the First World War." In fact, one of Laura's grandfathers (her father's father) had immigrated to America early in the twentieth century to avoid going into the Russian Army, which was torturous to Jews. Only to immediately enlist in the

U.S. Army and return to Europe where he had fought against the Germans (the Krauts, her father occasionally called them) in World War I.

Josef seemed to breathe a sigh of relief. Maybe her family's relatively long line of U.S. citizenship put her in a more safe class of Jew for him, one that might not hold an irrevocable grudge. Or so he can hope, thought Laura.

He continued, "The Jews have returned to Berlin. Most of them are Russians and know nothing of their heritage. Still, they are breathing new life into the old city. The Jews cannot be destroyed. I respect, I admire that."

Laura recalled the Turkish—and presumably Muslim—neighborhood that Byron had pointed out from the cab. She wondered how these immigrant populations coexisted in Berlin. Probably, in the post—9/11 world, the Jews were more tolerated than the Turks.

"Unlike those Russians, I grew up as an observant Jew. I still practice my religion," Laura said boldly.

"That is because you are an American. It is common there." He seemed nonplussed by her declaration. And why should he care? The Nazis had executed people whose parents had converted from Judaism and practiced Christianity. "The Russian Army invaded and defeated Hitler in this very city, in Berlin. I was sixteen years old at the time, making me one of the older members of what was left of the SS."

"The SS? Byron told me you were in the Hitler Youth." Laura looked at Byron. He had not said the SS, although maybe it had been implied.

A waiter arrived. They quickly surveyed the menus and made their selections. Josef ordered wine for the table.

"The SS?" Laura repeated.

"Yes. The Youth SS. It was sadly inevitable. Would you like to know more?"

Byron and Laura glanced at each other. "Yes. I would like to know more," said Laura.

"You will speak, Papa? After all this time?"

"I have found the right time."

"For Laura?"

"For the three of us."

The waiter returned with the bottle of wine. Its hue was nearly black. He poured a few drops into Josef's glass. Josef sampled the wine and gave his approval. The waiter filled all three glasses. Laura tried some. The wine was heavy and bitter. She preferred Beaujolais, but said nothing.

"It started when I was ten years old. I loved the regalia, the songs, and the games. Some of us even wore our uniforms to church, under our choir robes. We so looked forward to the meetings. My parents had their reservations, but allowed me to join because the Red Youth were thugs."

"The Red Youth?" questioned Laura.

"The Communist gangs," Josef replied. "They were brutal. They terrorized and murdered German children. Imagine Stalin as a midget multiplied many times over."

Laura laughed out loud. "Whatever." She had never before heard this rationalization of the Hitler Youth.

"It is well documented," Josef said. He drank some more wine. "My first sleepover trip was a milestone. My parents and I did not realize that the rigorous exercises performed during the day were military drills and that the tales told around the campfire at night, brainwashing.

"At night, we gathered around a fire and belted out patriotic songs. As I sang—my voice rising, my chest expanding, my lungs filling with air—I felt myself becoming a *man*.

"Our leader would entertain us with stories of demonic Jewish girls. He claimed that they had the power to seduce and devour us. I thought of one Jewish girl from my school, Tatiana, a Ukrainian émigré whose family had fled to Germany, escaping religious persecution. I thought she was beautiful. It was, as you call it, a double-edged sword.

I detested and desired, feared and revered the female Jew."

Like father, like son?

"When I returned to school that Monday, Tatiana was gone. All Jewish children had been banished."

Josef paused as the waiter placed bread and butter on the table. Byron and Laura did not touch it, but the elder Baumgaarten chomped on a roll.

"The East was far harsher in its treatment of Jews than Germany," Josef suddenly said.

"The East being . . .?"

"Poland," interjected Byron.

"Yes. The Poles cheered as the Jews were sent to the gas chambers. The real anti-Semitism was in Poland, the Ukraine, and the inferior, outer provinces. Germans are a refined people. Killing in their own backyards? I think not. The people to the East, the Poles, that is a whole other story."

A whole other story indeed, thought Laura . . . one that she was not buying. Byron was subtly nodding. He must be quite familiar with this version of history. One fact, Laura noted, was *irrefutable*. The United States had battled Germany, not Poland. Germany had been the enemy. Germany had started the war.

Was Laura—as an American born in 1960—similar to the veterans of World War II, a dying breed? One reason filmmaker Kenneth Burns had cited for making his documentary about WWII was that a preponderance of young Americans mistakenly believed that Americans and Germans had fought on the same side.

"For the record," Laura said, "Germany was our enemy in World War II."

"The real villain was Hitler. He tugged on the puppet strings of German society and blamed the Jews for all of its economic failures."

It sounded like age old, shopworn rhetoric. What did Josef truly believe and what had he done?

"Several years ago," she began bravely, "a book came out in

the United States. *Hitler's Willing Executioners.* It was quite controversial. Maybe you have heard of it?"

"No."

"The operative word being 'willing.'" She was trembling.

"Maybe my English is not so good."

"On the contrary, it is impeccable."

"My father was a career diplomat," said Byron. "He speaks six languages. He puts me to shame with my knowledge of three."

"German, English, and what is the third?"

"Romanian."

"Romanian? Why do you know Romanian?"

Byron looked uncomfortable and did not answer.

"Berlin has changed," said Josef. "I watch the Jews queuing up in front of the Jewish Museum. Some are Russians, flaunting their new religiousness with their skull caps and fringes hanging out from under their garments. Others are like you, blending into the populace. This is not the Holocaust Memorial, built by our government and steeped in controversy. This is *your* museum, Laura, built by *your* people, the Jews. You must see it. It is very affecting. Byron, you must take Laura."

Byron put down his glass of wine and said, "Absolutely. We will go."

Their previous visit to a Jewish museum, the one in Vienna, had culminated in sex. Hot sex.

"Yes, we will go," said Laura.

"I'm in," Byron reiterated and winked at her.

"Have you made the pilgrimage to a concentration camp?" asked Josef.

"No."

"Why not? Many Jewish tourists do this."

"Laura does not have to go to a concentration camp if she does not want to, Papa."

"I have gone," said Josef.

"You have?" Laura was surprised.

"Yes. I see your people holding up signs that bear the names of the deceased. Thousands of them coming from America, returning to the land of their lost loved ones. In my eyes, this parade is replaced by walking corpses. I see in their hollowed cheeks the moral void inherent in the attempt to destroy an entire race." He pounded on the table with both fists, rattling the dinnerware and Laura's nerves.

The food arrived. A fish with gold scales and an exposed eye lie flat on Josef's plate. It was decorated with parsley and accompanied by boiled potatoes. Laura's meal was angel hair pasta with olive oil, a bland dish that was not apt to cause havoc in her jittery stomach. Byron had ordered rack of lamb. The portion was fit for a prince.

Byron made a bib out of a big white cotton napkin. He held his cutlery over the meat and bones. "Let's eat," he said. "*Essen.*"

He seemed anxious to progress to the stately meal. He had probably heard all of this from his father before, the vaguely veiled anti-Semitism, the denial of historic facts. But what had Josef *done*?

Laura twirled the angel hair around her fork. Byron and Josef stared at her, mesmerized. They seemed to represent two generations of wunderlust. Was there even such a word? Not wanderlust, which was a zest for travel. Laura had that and then some. The German word she had coined was wunderlust, as in a powerful passion for sex. Upon her placing the buttery pasta in her mouth, father and son attacked their food.

They dined in silence. Josef quickly consumed the fish. His plate was spotless, save the fish's unblinking eyeball. Laura and Byron had not even finished half of their respective meals, when Josef resumed his speech.

"I often think of that girl. Her once lustrous brown eyes are now beacons of fear. I see her in a torn coat, weak and limping. She is my age, a playmate from my distant childhood, a shadow of her former self—"

"I told you that my father is quite the poet. When all else fails, he calls upon his romantic soul. Is this the mythical girl for whom you wrote the sonnet, Papa?"

"You have not heard this story."

"This is not new, Papa."

"You will see that it is."

All eyes, including the fish eyeball on the plate, were on Papa. Laura thought he was going to nudge it with a fork prong, causing it to roll around like a marble. He refrained. Was it out of respect for the whitefish that he had just gulped down? Did he equate Jews with a lowly species on the food chain?

"This was a real girl, Tatiana, from my school. I did not realize it at first. We were both fifteen years old, but she looked thirty-five. I recalled the lacy white socks that she used to wear and her strong tanned legs. Now I was staring at ripped tights and scraped skin.

"I had not seen her since her expulsion from our school. Before that, she had sat at the desk in front of mine. I remembered how her hair had cascaded down her back in spirals. I could not resist pulling on it, mainly because it made her turn around and look at me."

"Are you saying, Papa, that you were in love with a Jewish girl?"

"I—" Josef stammered. His eyes had grown misty.

"We call it puppy love," offered Laura.

"We were very young. And then I saw her, a few years later, about to be gassed."

"Papa, you—"

The busboy began clearing the table and Byron stopped in mid-sentence. Their waiter approached. "May I bring you something else, a cordial, perhaps?"

"No, thanks," replied Laura.

"Not for me," added Byron.

"Yes. I would like a hot tea with lemon and honey cake," said Josef.

"My pleasure, sir," said the waiter.

Laura noted that Josef had ordered the favorite dessert of her own father. She doubted that the two men had anything else in common.

"Papa, I did not know that you were at the camps."

"It was toward the end of the war when Hitler was running out of soldiers. He mandated that the boys join the SS. We had to go wherever they told us to go and do whatever they told us to do."

"And what if you refused?"

"Then I would have been executed. But rest assured. The Youth SS were but observers."

"Observers? Then why were you there?" Laura could not control her inquisitiveness.

"Do you mean, what was my complicity?"

"Of course that is what she means, Papa. It is what we both need to know."

"Then, I will tell you."

"Please tell us, Mr. Baumgaarten."

"I called her name. 'Tatiana,' I said. She jumped. I startled her. She was terrified that I was singling her out from the crowd. 'It is Josef from the school.' She did not seem to understand or hear or believe me, and continued to move with the herd. I had to do something. I followed her and pulled on her hair. It was brittle and thin, nothing like the luxuriant curls that I had remembered. I thought she would recognize me from this gesture, from our childhood.

"She began screaming. The protocol was for me to shoot her on the spot and walk away."

"I thought you were an observer."

"Yes, if unprovoked. If I did nothing, then another soldier would surely step in and gun her down."

"Your tea, sir." The waiter placed a silver teapot and tray before Josef.

"Ah, yes, thank you." With much pomp, Josef poured the tea into a fancy cup. While waiting for the steaming brew to cool, he continued. "I took her by the hand and led her away from the line. Instead of responding violently, as I had expected, she froze, which gave me the opportunity to whisper in her ear. 'It is *Josef* from school. From the *cheder*,' I emphasized."

"The *cheder*? That is the Hebrew word for school."

"I know. It came to me from out of nowhere. My survival instinct, I suppose. I led Tatiana to haystacks that were piled along the side of the road. I ordered her to get inside, to hide. When she was covered with hay, I fired shots into the stacks, being sure to aim away from Tatiana.

"I looked back over my shoulder. I saw the soldiers and the prisoners marching together, blurring as one, to the crematorium. 'Get out!' I said to Tatiana.

"She emerged from the hay. When her eyes met mine, I saw terror. Hatred. Confusion. 'Run!' I told her. She stumbled to her feet and started off.

"I stood there. I was paralyzed. Where would she go? Where would I go? I chased her and within moments, caught up. We ran together. I showed her a path into the woods. My boots crunched twigs and hardened snow. Tatiana's shoes were falling apart. Her feet were bleeding. I scooped her up and carried her in my arms. We continued until nightfall, when I was certain that we had escaped." Josef took a sip of tea.

"What became of Tatiana?" Byron asked. "Did she survive?"

"Yes."

"You saved her life," said Laura.

"Papa, why have you never told this story?"

"Your mother, my son. Now that she is gone, I can speak freely of my love for a Jewish girl."

CHAPTER 14:
ZSA ZSA

Byron was dubious. Why had Josef kept his heroism a secret for so many years? Certainly not for the sake of Byron's mother, who had been a loving and open-minded woman. She would have been proud of the courageous deed supposedly performed by her husband.

Why speak now? When conversing in German so that Laura would not understand, Josef had promised his son that he would do everything possible to put his lovely new girlfriend at ease. Byron knew that with his propensity for poetry and drama, Josef was capable of dreaming up a convincing story for Laura's benefit. It sounded real, but was it true?

Regardless, "Dinner with Papa" had been a success. It had had a positive impact on Byron's relationship with Laura. In her mind anyway, Josef had redeemed himself. She no longer seemed tense in that typically stressed out American way.

She had stopped expressing to him her guilt for romping about with the son of a Nazi. What *he* was keeping from *her* was his deeply profound shame. *His* people had committed the heinous crimes upon *her* people. This was incontrovertible.

They were in the east end of Berlin, in an emergent gallery that specialized in brash, juvenile works. It was the ideal space for Sergei's sculptures. Laura was lounging on one of the cheesy sofas. Her blonde hair half shielded the face that he oftentimes wanted to eat up. At this moment, he thought she looked fourteen. If he tore off her clothes, it would immediately dispel that silly perception. She was all woman. When they discussed serious topics, such as politics and world affairs, she seemed her age, forty-five. It was a joy and a relief to be with someone who was his contemporary and equal.

Most of all, he loved her sense of adventure. It was equal to his. They had planned (and packed for) a two-day trip and already they had been away for five days. What a whirlwind journey it was.

Yesterday, they had gone shopping for more clothes for Laura. He subtly guided her to the lingerie section of a department store in the west end of Berlin. She picked out a beige slip with ivory lace. She said it could be a dress. Who was he to argue?

"It's a Vera Wang," she noted. "She does these amazing wedding gowns."

In spite of this *huge hint*, Byron felt blissful. Maybe someday, he would marry her.

Stranger things had happened to him.

She was wearing the lingerie now. Its rosy flesh color matched the tonality of her skin. He took her hand and got ready to lift her from the couch. There was a bag from the Berlin outpost of Urban Outfitters. She had explored the city while Byron had met with the gallery owner.

She asked him, "Were you successful?"

"Yes, very. This place is perfect for Sergei. Don't you agree?"

"I do."

He pulled on her hand and she stood up. She took the plastic shopping bag in her free hand. As they were crossing the threshold to go outside—still hand in hand—Byron came face to face with a face from his past, one he preferred to forget.

Her long black hair framed the familiar high cheekbones and jutting square jaw. In that very first instant, he almost did not recognize her due to a set of new, big, black-framed eyeglasses.

"Zsa Zsa?"

"Byron?" When she took off her glasses, Byron thought her face looked puffier than before. She must be thirty-five by now.

Zsa Zsa blocked the exit. Enough of this, Byron thought. He started to brush past her. In her typical manner, Zsa Zsa did not yield.

"Zsa Zsa, this is Laura." He moved back, allowing an area in which to present his new girlfriend to his ex. "Laura, this is Zsa Zsa."

"Hi," said Laura.

"Hello."

"We were on our way out," said Byron.

"I can see that. What are you doing in Berlin?"

"What are *you* doing in Berlin?"

"I live here," she replied.

"You live here? No kidding." He was genuinely surprised. Regaining his composure, he quipped, "So, you have said *reverdere* to *Bucuresti?*"

"Yes, you can say that, yes. What about you?"

"Laura and I are traveling."

"Just traveling?" She shot an insinuating look at Laura.

"Byron is showing me around Europe," said Laura. "I am taking a break from my career. I used to work in advertising."

"Did you? How nice."

"Laura is from the United States, too."

"Obviously . . . " She turned her attention back to Byron. "Where is home for you now? Do you have a permanent base?"

Byron had hoped he could avoid this question. He was not sure he wanted Zsa Zsa to be able to track him down. As he hesitated, Laura jumped in. "We do," she said. "We both live in Prague."

"Both?" She seemed to be angling for more information, as if asking, "Do you live together?" When neither Byron nor Laura responded to her probe, she exclaimed in her natural Texan drawl, "Welcome to Berlin. Or, in your case, Byron, welcome *back* to Berlin. Allow me to show you some real East German hospitality."

She was loosening up, which Byron knew could spell trouble.

"Let's all go somewhere where we can get better acquainted or reacquainted, shall we? Are you game?" Zsa Zsa was looking at Byron as if it were a dare.

He met her gaze with silence. He recognized the impulse to reject this woman. It would be both easy and complicated to say no. He had rebuffed her years ago, in a particularly cruel way. It was when she was a rising performance artist and he was a condemning art critic. It felt natural to do it to her all over again. Worse, he was concerned with the multi-dimensionality of the word "it."

"I know of a café on the river. It's only a few blocks from here. We can catch up," Zsa Zsa suggested. "What do you say, Byron?"

An excuse eluded him. They had no other plans for the evening. Unlike his father, Byron was incapable of ad-libbing a story. Besides, agreeing to this one quick outing with Zsa Zsa would assuage the guilt he felt for having once dumped her and finally set things right. At least, this is what he tried to tell himself.

Yet he knew it was his ravenous quest for adventure that made him turn to his present girlfriend and ask, "What do you say, Laura?"

*

Laura fixed a smile on her face. "Sure, why not?"

On the short walk over, Zsa Zsa offered up everything Laura could possibly wish to know about her. That is, everything except for the details regarding Zsa Zsa's relationship with Byron. Zsa Zsa was originally from the Dallas-Fort Worth Metroplex. In 1996, she transplanted herself to Bucharest. Her family had fled the ancestral city between the two World Wars. Zsa Zsa was not her real name, but "homage to the legendary actress, Zsa Zsa Gabor." No matter that Gabor was Hungarian and Zsa Zsa II was Romanian. In art circles, Zsa Zsa became known as "The Cindy Sherman of Bucharest."

"Cindy Sherman is now considered one of the greatest artists of our generation," declared Zsa Zsa. "Do you know who she is?"

"Uh-huh." Laura thought Zsa Zsa was being condescending.

"She was a pioneer, the first to subvert pop culture symbols. Going beyond Cindy, I acted out the not mutually exclusive archetypes of a vagrant Romanian woman and a sexy stray cat prowling the grand boulevards of Bucharest."

It sounded convoluted, yet Laura was admittedly impressed.

"One reviewer—who shall remain *nameless*—accused me of, quote, appropriating the appropriated, of being derivative to the nth degree, unquote. Does any of this make sense to you? Do you get his drift?"

"I think so. It sounds harsh."

"Who would write such drivel?" asked Byron. Zsa Zsa glared at him, but then followed through with a seductive smile.

They arrived at the riverside café. The three of them sat down at an intimate table, suitable for two. In the waning golden light, Laura took in Zsa Zsa's copious black hair and violet eyes. She looked to Laura like a gypsy, and perhaps she was. The Romanies were gypsies. Were Romanies and Romanians one and the same? She had no idea. Byron had told her the other night that he was fluent in three languages, English, German, and Romanian. She had asked him why Romanian, but could not recall his reply, if there had been one. Now Laura knew why. He had, at some undisclosed time in his past, spoken Romanian to this tigress.

Why had he not tactfully turned down her invitation?

Then, remembering the bizarre love triangle in Bratislava, Laura wondered if Byron was hoping for another threesome, this time with Zsa Zsa.

In close proximity, Zsa Zsa reeked of meat. Laura guessed it was venison or wild boar consumed the night before. Under a dark, linty blazer, she wore a diaphanous top. She possessed bulbous knockers, the tops of which poured out of her formidable bra. Laura also was able to observe her rib cage and remarkably narrow waist.

She lit a cigarette and blew smoke. Laura waved it away, flashing her seashell pink manicure. In contrast, there was dirt beneath Zsa Zsa's fingernails. More smoke encircled the head of this snake charmer. Laura thought she gave off the false airs of having endured the brutalities of Romanian dictator, Ceausescu (Zsa Zsa had entered the country after his reign).

Laura tried to imagine Zsa Zsa growing up in Texas. With her untamed appearance, she must have been a social outcast among the coifed and waxed Dallas debs. Laura recalled her own wholesome teenaged years. She had been widely accepted and popular in high school. In Eastern Europe, the All-American Girl could be pretty exotic. Hang on to that thought, Laura told herself. You may need it to buttress yourself against what comes next.

"You never did tell me what brings you to Berlin. How are your parents?"

"My mother died two years ago," answered Byron.

"I'm sorry."

"Thank you. My father is his usual self."

"Was that his usual self?" asked Laura. She thought his confessional had been anything but usual.

"We had dinner with him the other night. He was in top form, as always. But our real reason for coming here is I am representing a new artist—"

"That's right. I'd heard you'd made the switch from criticism to sales. That's quite a three-sixty."

"One-eighty," Laura quietly corrected her.

"It is true that I am selling. Yet I am also helping young artists build their reputations. It is very gratifying."

"I am sure it is. Is it more satisfying than slamming their work?"

Byron frowned. "Yes, of course it is, Zsa Zsa."

Laura was getting the distinct impression that these two shared a discordant past. Had they been lovers? Had he ever called her his *Geliebte?*

Zsa Zsa removed from her leather shoulder bag a laptop computer. She turned it on. "Do you mind if I show you something from my portfolio? It just so happens that I am between agents."

Zsa Zsa adjusted the position of the screen so that all three of them could get a good look. Laura was shocked by what she saw. It was a video of a scantily clad, writhing Zsa Zsa. She was basically pole dancing with images of the Eiffel Tower, the Washington Monument—the not so subtle phallic symbols of the Western World—and Michelangelo's David.

The onscreen Zsa Zsa was spinning like a top. The force of her cyclonic movements caused each of the manmade icons to detonate and disperse in rapid succession. She triumphantly resurfaced from the swirling dust and debris, recalling Botticelli's Venus rising from a clamshell.

As Zsa Zsa looked up from the video, Laura envied her. It was not only for her past liaison with Byron, whatever that may be. It was also for the obvious pride she took in her work. It made Laura wistful for her own career, even if it had never been as audacious and narcissistic as this.

Byron gulped and his eyes watered. "Where do I sign?"

"I'm supposed to be asking you that question." Zsa Zsa laughed.

"You're right." He removed papers from his bag. "You have earned yourself a new agent, Zsa Zsa. *Felicitari!*"

"*Multumesc!*" Zsa Zsa beamed.

A pang of jealousy stabbed Laura. Zsa Zsa turned to her. "He congratulated me and I thanked him in Romanian."

"I got that."

They stood up to say goodbye. Zsa Zsa and Byron embraced to seal the deal. Just before they separated, Byron whispered something in Zsa Zsa's ear.

Then Zsa Zsa startled Laura by lingeringly kissing her on both cheeks.

Zsa Zsa departed, heading down a path along the river and disappearing into what was now the night. *There will be no threesome*, thought Laura. She exhaled a sigh of relief and felt, strangely, regret.

CHAPTER 15:
THE PLAGUES

Their five-star hotel room overlooked designer boutiques on the *Kurfürstendamm*, a West Berlin boulevard that reminded Laura of a faded Paris. It had been three days since they had checked in. By now, Laura was familiar with many of the hotel employees. It was her nature to be friendly to them and they responded by treating her like the resident princess. She was going to miss the pampering.

After the episode with Zsa Zsa, Laura and Byron had returned to the hotel for a brief rest before going out again for dinner. She was on the bed still wearing the beige Vera Wang undergarment when Byron held up a black slip.

"This is your dress's evil twin," he declared. "Change into it."

"It looks punk." It was slashed with holes.

Laura put it on and looked in the mirror. The holes were in tactical locations, allowing glimpses of her breasts and belly. Laura was not sure if she looked sexy or ridiculous. She felt both, simultaneously.

"Perfect," remarked Byron. He was holding a tube of shocking pink lipstick. It seemed surreal in his hand. It had better be for her and not him. "Hold still. I'll do it."

He carefully applied the lipstick to her mouth. He stepped back to survey his work. "Superb," he said.

He grabbed a cell phone recharger cable and tied it around her wrist. As he took a few steps away from Laura, he tugged on the cord and caused it to tighten. Obviously, her boyfriend liked seeing her trussed up. But for what and for whom?

He went to the closet and got her trench coat, which he draped over her shoulders like a cape. "If we are going out in public, then you must be decent."

"You call this decent?"

"That will be up to us."

"I need shoes." She was standing in her bare feet.

"You're right. The restaurant will not admit you without them."

Her stilettos were beside the bed. He positioned her feet inside of them. As he laced up the high-heeled sandals, he caressed her lower legs. Laura longed for him to keep going, higher. Dinner could wait.

"Ready?" he asked.

He did not wait for her response. He pulled her out of the room, down the hallway, and to the elevator by tugging on the wire. Every so often, he looked back at Laura. She felt like his property.

The elevator arrived. A Japanese family already occupied it. Laura considered letting the car continue downward without the two of them, but Byron directed her inside. Laura supposed she looked like a flasher. Next to Laura stood a small Japanese girl and a slightly older boy, their cute faces inches away from her trench coat and bare legs.

The woman frowned at her. She placed one hand over the face of each child, masking their eyes. The man, presumably her husband, could not take *his* eyes off Laura.

Finally, the elevator reached the main floor and the doors opened.

"Whore," muttered the Japanese woman in English with no trace of an accent as the family scurried out.

Byron proceeded across the lobby, dragging her as if she were a dog on a leash. It was difficult keeping up with him in her high heels on the slippery floor. The trench coat, due to it being unbuttoned at the collar, slid off her shoulders. Laura stood exposed in front of the cheerful employees at the front desk.

"Here you are, Miss." A bellhop retrieved her coat. He assisted her in putting it on properly, with her arms through the sleeves.

The cable was stretched across the lobby. Byron pulled on it. "Come along, *Geliebte*."

"Have a nice time, Miss," said the bellhop. Laura followed Byron to the revolving doors. The doorman twice tipped his hat at them. "Good evening, Sir. Good evening, Miss. Enjoy your night."

In the cab, Byron told the driver the address and then said to Laura, "We're going to Hell."

"What?" Laura questioned, mildly annoyed. The bondage and exhibitionism were his doing. She did not like that he was now implying that they would face eternal damnation for it.

"The name of the restaurant is Hell."

In Hell, a flight of stairs led to the main dining area. On the way down, they passed a diorama of reptiles. One lizard extended a split red tongue. Was this for real or a mechanical device? Why put the patrons on edge? Perhaps that was the point, thought Laura, already nostalgic for a kinder and gentler Prague.

The dining room was reassuringly provincial, with its white tablecloths and flickering candles. Byron led her to their reserved table. As she squeezed within the narrow space between their table and the wall, she became aware for the first time of bristly pubic hairs growing back. Ugh.

Now what? Triple ugh. 1) She could let them grow out and endure excruciating itchiness. 2) She could avoid that ordeal by shaving every day. 3) She could let the stubble grow enough for it to be yanked out in an extreme bikini wax. Yes, Laura decided, that was what she would do, as soon as they got home. To Prague, that is. She would combine it with a long overdue leg waxing. Amidst all of the recent excitement, she was no longer the most well groomed person in the world. Byron did not seem to mind.

Just as she was foreseeing a Czech cosmetologist applying beeswax to her pea pod, she heard Byron say, "Zsa Zsa! What a surprise!"

There she was, at *their* table, looking a hundred times more sanitized than she had an hour or two ago.

Zsa Zsa's midnight tresses were piled on top of her head in an elaborate bouffant. It was the same hairdo once worn by Zsa Zsa Gabor, although the famous actress was a platinum blonde. Zsa

Zsa II wore teardrop rhinestone earrings and a clingy red dress with plunging neckline.

Byron sat down next to Zsa Zsa and across from Laura. Had this meeting been orchestrated? Zsa Zsa and Byron were eyeing her appreciatively. What exactly was going on here? While Laura was ten years older than Zsa Zsa, she was being made to feel as if she were with . . . her *parents!* Memories rushed over her like waves on a sandy shore. It had been a long time since Laura had been in the happy company of both her parents. Her mother had died seven years ago.

It was too weird. Laura distracted herself by reading the menu. She was grateful that in Hell, the Devil had seen fit to present the selections in English. Unfortunately, everything on the menu included pork ingredients. That settled it. The Jews were not going to Hell.

"I can't eat anything on this menu." Laura was mortified when she heard her voice. She sounded like a whimpering girl.

"I am sure there is something you can eat." Zsa Zsa winked at her.

Yes, but not with you around. An uncorked bottle of wine was on the table. Byron poured the amethyst liquid into all three glasses. He raised his chalice. Zsa Zsa did the same.

In rebellion, Laura did not lift her glass. Her mind went to the Kosher Manischevitz wine served at the Passover table. She recalled the tradition of dipping her pinkie finger in the wine and releasing ten droplets on her clean plate. Each drop was for one of the Ten Plagues. All Ten Plagues had afflicted the Egyptians, but *passed over* the Jews. The first plague was blood. Laura had a premonition that before the evening was over, she would see blood.

"Are you going to join us?" Byron asked.

She looked up at him. The second plague was frogs, wads of them, more than one could comprehend. Was her prince a frog, unable to contain his desire for more than one woman?

"You look deep in thought," he added.

Vermin. Locusts. Hail. She silently ticked off each plague: A Night of Utter Darkness, an especially terrifying curse. The

Egyptians had been unable to see anything. Wherever they looked, an impenetrable black void was before them. How would *this* night end?

Boils, thought Laura, the scourge of acne when you are a *high school reject*. She projected this vile plague diagonally across the table to Zsa Zsa. She could do this. She could transcend her jealousy.

"I apologize. My mind was wandering." She lifted her glass.

"To new adventures," said Byron. The three goblets clinked. Laura set hers back down on the table without taking a sip.

"Drink up," said Zsa Zsa.

The other woman's powdery face and noir rimmed violet eyes shimmered seductively in the candlelight.

A little alcohol might boost my self-confidence, thought Laura. She inserted the rim of the glass between her bright pink lips, letting her blonde hair fall across her face. From under hooded eyes, she gazed up at Byron. "What does this remind you of, Byron?"

"That's more like it. That's my Laura."

"To new adventures," she said in a husky voice that was new to her.

Laura gulped the wine.

Her body grew warm. It was time to take off the trench coat and be an adult. She shrugged out of it. Now she felt her holed dress was lascivious and not at all ludicrous.

She saw herself as the object of both of their desires. In the presence of these two other, worldlier individuals—one the product of Swiss schooling and a prosperous postwar Germany, the other with her sophisticated, decadent pretensions—Laura perceived that she was the quintessential girl-girl.

She took another huge swallow of wine. It floated down her throat and filled her tummy. Byron got up from his chair and in doing so, pulled on the electrical cord that connected them. It signaled to Laura that the two of them were a couple. He joined her on the bench seat and put his arm around her. She felt secure and protected, but was she?

"You make a cute couple," Zsa Zsa said.

"We make a spectacular couple," said Byron.

"We make a *speck tack couple.* That could be one word. That's so German of me." Laura giggled. "It's like wienerwurst. In English, it's two short words, hot dog. In German, it is one long word with all of its syllables smashed together. This is what Heidegger and Hegel did." What the hell was Laura talking about? And from what reservoir of memories had these two German philosophers emerged? She herself must be smashed. That, or utterly fixated on Byron's own adorable hot dog. The room was starting to spin.

"You make perfect sense," said Byron.

"She does?" asked Zsa Zsa.

"What did you put in this drink? Something, no doubt, to render me completely inarticulate." It was not as if Laura was the master—or mistress, as it were—of articulation. When she was with Byron, it was often the opposite. At this moment, however, she felt supremely intelligent. Hey, she was no airhead, even if a girlie girl. Now, if only she could spout (or remember!) Hegel. From Philo101, she should be able to cite the famous chapter from Phenomenology of Mind, the one upon which Marx devised his theory of the overthrow of capitalism. It had to do with the master and the slave. The slave frees herself from her shackles and becomes the dominatrix of a new underclass. Those know-it-all German minds of the eighteenth and nineteenth centuries had not bothered to deconstruct how Moses had led the Jews from slavery to freedom or attempted to explain the miracle parting of the Red Sea. What would it be like for Laura to turn the tables on Byron and Zsa Zsa, who seemed to exert a subtle superiority and control over her?

"Or to render you utterly unresisting." That was Byron speaking.

She had the legs and arms and neck of a jellyfish. She slid down on the bench, resting her head on his lap. He deliberately tugged on the wiring, tied about her wrist. She loved this . . . and him.

Her position—face down on his crotch—was reminiscent of their train ride to Bratislava. Or had it been to Vienna? Budapest? They had quite a storied past, the two of them, and it was still in the making! He stroked her hair with a warm palm and spoke in hushed tones to Zsa Zsa. That Laura should be wearing a studded dog collar was the final thought that wafted through her consciousness before she fell asleep.

CHAPTER 16:
THE APOCALYPSE

Where was she? When Laura woke up, she was utterly disoriented. She had the sense that she was suspended. The first thing she saw below (or was it above?) her was a bed and a black and red tiled floor (or was it the ceiling?). On the walls, there were upside down murals, depicting an inverted New York skyline. The recognizable Empire State and Chrysler Buildings were pointed downwards and the East River flowed above them. The Twin Towers had been respectfully omitted from the scene.

As she gradually came to and got her bearings, Laura discovered that she was lying in a recessed space below the floorboards. The room had been intentionally designed to appear upside down. The bed was above her, apparently glued to the ceiling. The blue sky and puffy clouds were painted near the room's baseboards.

"I don't think I am in Hell anymore. Worse."

"Is this not to your liking?" Zsa Zsa stood looking down at her.

"No. Where am I?"

"You are in Room 23 of the Apocalypse Hotel. It is also known as the Upside Down Room."

"Zsa Zsa knows the manager," she heard Byron say.

"I performed here for the grand opening."

"If Laura does not like this room, you can show her something else, right Zsa Zsa?"

"Yes. Room 17 is also available. I have the master key."

Laura climbed out. Her wrists were tied together with the battery charger cable. She was no longer tethered to Byron. He took her hands and helped her up. She still had on that sleazy black slip he had made her wear. How long had she been asleep?

Days? Hours? It felt like minutes.

"What time is it?"

"Ten or thereabouts," he said.

Laura and Byron followed Zsa Zsa out of the Upside Down Room and down the hall. Zsa Zsa stopped and unlocked a door.

"Voilà! The Room of Mirrors."

They went inside. There were mirrors upon mirrors, reflections of reflections. It was like being in the center of a chiseled ice cube. As Laura turned her head, her image moved in parallel. She was not able to gaze directly at her own eyes. It was disconcerting.

Zsa Zsa led Laura to a round bed. The hotelier had probably purchased it from IKEA, thought Laura, recognizing it from an in-store display. The Sultan, it was called. It was difficult to imagine how it might accommodate three people. Where there's a will, there's a—

Zsa Zsa pushed Laura down on the bed.—Way! As soon as she did, Laura felt a rush of adrenaline. Was it anger? Was it the humiliation of being treated as a rag doll, unable to push back due to her clasped hands?

No. It was neither. Laura realized that it was desire! She felt wet and tingly. She watched Zsa Zsa remove the hairpins from her upsweep. The black pelt fell on her mole spotted shoulders. Her hair was matted with spray and resembled a scouring pad.

Laura could make out Zsa Zsa's nipples and ribcage beneath the stretchy red dress. It was obvious from an area of bumpy texture that she was not wearing any underwear and that no one had taken the razor to *her*. Had Byron discovered this first hand *with his hand* while sitting next to Zsa Zsa in Hell?

She turned her head to look for him. Reflections of this movement rippled throughout the room. Where was Byron? She saw his mirrored images, but where was *he?* Where was his corporeality? Nothing had happened . . . yet. She could still tell him that she wanted to leave.

Zsa Zsa's breasts dangled above her. Her butt was in the air.

Byron ought to spank her! Take that, bitch! Just then, he came over to her. He kissed Laura hard on the mouth and pulled on her tangled, golden hair. It hurt. No. Not me. Punish *her.*

As he aggressively pushed his tongue into her, Laura immediately yielded to him. She was all his. She belonged to Byron.

A hand glided between her thighs and immediately found her hot, pulsating slit. It felt luscious, those fingers skating over her most prized erotic zone. Oh! It was so unbelievable. Yes, Laura had done this to herself, and had had it done to her, countless times in the past. But it had never felt like this. And then she had a horrifying (and, in the recesses of her mind, titillating) realization. Only a woman could know so much about another woman. She was being clit teased by Zsa Zsa!

Perplexingly, the gross-out factor served to excite her even more. Laura arched her back, aching to be taken by both her male and female lovers.

Frustrating Laura, they both moved away from her. She gazed up at the mirrored ceiling and at her own longing, abandoned image. The fuchsia lipstick exaggerated her mouth. Her blonde hair was smashed against the pillow. Her body was strewn on a white duvet. The bottom part of the black slip was stuck between her thighs. A single breast poked through one of the strategically cut holes.

"Beautiful Laura," Byron said hoarsely.

Zsa Zsa did not say anything. She disappeared briefly and returned with a pair of scissors.

She inserted the pointed tips of the closed scissors between Laura's thighs. It occurred to Laura that Zsa Zsa might use them on her as a dildo. Thankfully, Zsa Zsa did not. Rather, she opened the scissors and snipped, starting at the bottom of Laura's dress. She continued until she sliced through it entirely. The garment fell away, revealing all of Laura, naked and vulnerable.

When the evening was over, she would have nothing to wear but a trench coat. It seemed like a minor detail at this point.

They told her to stand up, which she did. Zsa Zsa put one of her fingers on Laura's lips.

"Taste it."

Laura was reluctant.

"Don't worry. It's you."

Laura tasted Zsa Zsa's finger. It was salty. She felt queasy.

"It was me," Zsa Zsa said triumphantly. Zsa Zsa's tone disturbed her. Implicit in the affirmation that it had been Zsa Zsa stroking her to near orgasm was its negation—that it had *not* been Byron. And Zsa Zsa seemed to be implying that *that* was in and of itself meaningful. But what did it mean? Were his feelings for Laura second rate? Was he saving his best moves for Zsa Zsa?

A basket case! Yes, that was what she was becoming . . . and inexplicably aroused. As if on autopilot, she untied Zsa Zsa's halter straps. No one had asked her to do this. She was moved by, if not passion, then curiousness. Was this what Byron wanted? Was he waiting for his two girls to go at it with each other in unbridled feline heat? Was he using Laura to get a full view of Zsa Zsa's killer bod? Laura was not so naïve to presume that Byron actually needed her for this. Would this be his first time viewing?

The untied halter straps rested on Zsa Zsa's shoulders. Her ample bosom managed to keep the dress in place.

Byron removed his pants and boxer shorts, revealing his cock. It was larger than Laura had ever seen it. She wanted to tell Byron that he was "phantasmagoric," but could not pronounce the multisyllabic word in her dazed state.

Zsa Zsa got behind Laura and expertly massaged Laura's breasts. In spite of her misgivings, Laura felt more stimulated. She thought, *I'm disgusting*, while doing nothing to stop Zsa Zsa. She liked it. Then, Zsa Zsa hoisted Laura—who was the much smaller and lighter of the two women—above the ground. She positioned Laura for Byron to take aim at her.

She looked past him, at their reflections in the mirrors. Byron still had on his Oxford shirt, but was naked from the waist down. Laura herself appeared fractured and elongated in the mirrors, like a woman in the Picasso masterpiece, "The Demoiselles (translation: the Whores) of Avignon." She waited for him to come toward her, reach for her hips, pull her to him and—

Without warning, Zsa Zsa released Laura from her grip. Laura's feet landed on the floor with a thud.

Zsa Zsa took off her red dress. She tossed it on the floor next to Laura. It spread like a pool of blood.

Blood: The first of the ten plagues.

Zsa Zsa stepped forward and planted herself next to Laura.

Laura could not look up at her. She gazed down instead at Zsa Zsa's reflection in the mirrored floor. The other woman possessed the calf muscles of a triathlon athlete. Her thighs appeared compressed. The single point perspective of this composition drew Laura to the image she most dreaded, Zsa Zsa's dense and unruly black bush.

Laura stole a glance at the real, undistorted Zsa Zsa, who stood at her side. From the projectile nipples and mushrooming areolas to the extraordinary sway of her curvy hips, every detail of Zsa Zsa made Laura feel waiflike—and insignificant—by comparison.

No one moved. Perhaps out of duty as the only man in the room, Byron reached out and tentatively touched one of Zsa Zsa's—

Aaahhh! A scream went off inside of Laura's head.

In slow motion, Byron firmly grasped Zsa Zsa's boobs. Those hands! Yet were they not three consenting adults? There were worse things, right? Like what?!? Like falling prey to the murderous hands of the Nazis, that's what. Had he set her up for this all along? Had he from the start planned to seduce and then degrade her? Was it because she was Jewish? Yes, that must be it!

The reflections of Zsa Zsa and Byron were everywhere. She could not escape from looking at them. She felt like throwing up. She could only *leave*.

Where was her trench coat? She had no backpack and no

clothes, only this stupid cell phone wire tied around her wrists. She bit into it and loosened it with her teeth, freeing her hands. Then she spotted her filthy trench coat lying languidly on a chair. She threw it on, grabbed her shoes, and darted out the door.

She would not look back. She would not torment herself with what she might see. The two of them, their bodies locked in rapture, him above her and drilling her to oblivion—

"Laura, wait!" Byron called after her.

Down the hallway, she came to a door that was ajar. She pushed at it, thinking it might be an exit. Instead, it was another screwy bedchamber where a mature couple, maybe in their sixties, slept in his 'n' her coffins. What kind of wacky hotel was this? Who would pay money to stay in this fun house that was no fun at all?

Byron chased her down the hall. He had put back on his boxers. When had he taken off his shirt? What had transpired in the short span of time since she had left the room?

Realizing that all of her vital belongings—her credit cards, money, and passport—were locked in the safe in their room at the other, *the sane,* hotel, she said, "I need some money."

"You don't have to run away. I will take you back to the hotel. Without that woman," he added.

"No. Stay here with Zsa Zsa." The name hissed against her teeth as she said it.

"I'm sorry, Laura. I made a big mistake. I thought you were having a good time."

"You call this a good time? I don't think so."

She fought back tears. The image of the bedraggled, blonde girl in the Viennese jail cell flashed through her mind. Knowing her had been an omen. She had reminded Laura of a younger version of herself. It was now clear why: They were both barefoot, beggars, and, to differing degrees, trapped.

How could he have done this to her? And why had she let him? She stood immobile in a circle of numbness, staring at Byron in disbelief. She knew that she had to leave him, but how? After all they had been through—including their declarations of love—how could she ever leave him?

The solution presented itself in the form of her former cellmate. Embodying that girl's young and raging soul, Laura pushed Byron into the Coffin Room and ran away.

CHAPTER 17:
STREET URCHIN REDUX

She bolted down the staircase. With each step, she felt she was defining the future: She was giving up Byron forever. In her heart, she was crying for him. Her body was exhibiting more intelligence and will than her emotions, and kept her moving relentlessly.

Once outside, she knew she was lost. Where in Berlin was she? She had been asleep—or more accurately, comatose or out of her mind, Laura scolded herself—when abducted to this secret location.

She had no map. Irregular shadows blotted the desolate side street, due to low hanging tree branches. A deafening, screeching alarm suddenly went off. It made Laura think she should be heading for a bomb shelter. An emergency light flashed over someone's garage.

She ran down the sidewalk to what she hoped would be a busy thoroughfare. The traffic here was disappointingly sparse. There were no cabs in sight. A rattling truck clanged over a manhole. A beat-up sedan lumbered by, its driver twisting his head out the window to gawk at her. Across the street, there was a dark, dense park so dripping with menace it made Laura think of a gooey Black Forest Cake.

A night of utter darkness: Yet another plague.

What if she were again kidnapped, this time with truly dire consequences? Where was Byron? It was sinking in that he was not coming after her. If only he would call out her name. Instead, all she heard was that annoying siren.

She jogged for a few blocks to another side street. This one was residential and possibly safe, although graffiti was sprayed on the sides of the homes. A woman dressed in rags sorted through a packed shopping cart. Her legs were charcoaled and ballooned. Laura realized that since arriving in Europe, she had not seen a bag lady until now.

That will be me someday, thought Laura: A bag lady clinging to all of her *stuff* as a means of protecting herself from a brutal world. Laura needed *her* stuff so that she could return to Prague. Abused, haunted by the memories of her man rejecting her for a rival woman—

"I am not insignificant!" Laura suddenly shouted at the bag lady, who continued to paw through all of her esteemed belongings, unfazed by Laura.

"I—am—not—insignificant!" Laura again screamed, the words scratching against her throat, bellowing down the road. They were to Laura an anthem of sisterhood. Nevertheless, they elicited no reaction from the bag lady.

Maybe I *am* insignificant, thought Laura.

No. "I am *not* insignificant," she repeated in a subdued voice.

*

"Laura! Laura!" Byron called out her name. An emergency siren drowned out his cries. She was nowhere in sight. How could she have disappeared so swiftly? He ran down the road, pausing to peer down the narrow alleyways that separated some of the buildings.

What have I done? He loved Laura. Then why had he not resisted the temptation of being with two women? His plan (and Zsa Zsa's, damn her) had been to make Laura feel desired. He had broadly miscalculated. *What is wrong with me?*

Byron had grown up not far away from here. This block—with its dingy houses, wild shrubbery, and littered sidewalks—had degenerated. He pictured a cloaked man, lurking in one of those dark alleys and assailing Laura with a knife.

If something bad happened to her, he would never forgive himself.

He reached an occupied avenue and glanced about in all directions. Cars and buses passed in front of him. There were smatterings of people, but no Laura. His heart sank.

*

Laura reached a boulevard that looked vaguely familiar. Much to her relief, there were cabs. She dangled one of her stilettos. A taxi swerved to the curb. She slid into its back seat. The driver was a senior white male. Laura assumed he was working to supplement a meager pension. He had a bent nose. She could picture him crouched over a sandwich. It would be corned beef on a poppy seed roll.

"Do you speak English?" Laura inquired.

"Nein. Kein Englisch."

Laura had no idea where they were going. How would she pay him? She was presently penniless.

The driver had one hand on the steering wheel. He was wearing a short-sleeved shirt. There was a tattoo on his forearm just above his wrist. It was grayish green and had hatch marks. The Nazis had branded the Jews, knowing that Judaism prohibited tattoos. The man must have been a young boy when captured by the Germans. How had he survived? What had been the fates of his mama and his papa, his brothers and sisters if he had had any? And why had he decided to stay or return here, to Berlin, after the war?

"I have no money, no Euros," she said sadly. Laura started to leave the cab.

The driver waved her back inside. "Iz okay," he said.

"I will pay you when we get to the hotel."

He looked back at her without comprehending. "Hotel?"

She did not remember the name of the hotel. How would she communicate to him which one? "Yes. It's a very *big* hotel. Very grand. And ritzy."

"Ritzy?"

"Yes."

"*Das* Ritz?"

"No. I don't think so." It was not the Ritz Carlton.

"*Das* Kempi?" the driver asked.

"What? I don't know."

"*Das* Kempi!" He punched the steering wheel, accidentally honking the horn and nodding yes to his own question. He confidently put on his turn signal and got back into the traffic. Within minutes, they were in the nice part of town. They pulled up to the front of the hotel, The Kempinksi. Laura immediately recognized it. Well-heeled Berliners and tourists were enjoying late night cocktails on the sidewalk terrace.

She told the cab driver to wait. "Stay here. Don't go away. I will be right back with the money, *with the Euros.*"

A doorman greeted Laura. "Good evening, Miss. Welcome back. *Herr* Baumgaarten? Where might he be?"

Laura saw that the driver was pulling up to the taxi stand for his next fare. "Do you see that cabdriver? Please tell him not to leave. I am going up to my room to get some money so I can pay him."

Laura did not have a key. She told the concierge. One of the bellhops gladly accompanied her to the room. She skirted inside and went straight for the safe. The combination was 731, easily remembered, as July 31 was her brother's birthday. She grabbed the envelope that contained her Euros. Back downstairs, Laura was relieved to see that the cabdriver was still there.

"Thank you so much for waiting." She handed him twenty Euros, which was double the amount she owed him. He reached into his pocket for change and she told him no. In Europe, it was customary to tip by rounding up to the nearest Euro, which Laura felt represented a stingy percentage. This man was a Holocaust survivor and Laura had been cavorting with the enemy. Whatever she gave him, it would not erase his tragic youth. He stared back at her with soggy, drooping eyes.

Laura dreaded going back upstairs to the hotel room, *their* room. She did not want to be reminded of the intimacy they had shared. Where else could she go?

Josef (of all people!) had recommended to her Berlin's Jewish Museum. He had said, "This is *your* museum, built by *your* people. You must see it. Byron, you must take Laura." He had also mentioned Germany's new Holocaust Memorial. Unfortunately, both would be closed.

Dejectedly, she returned to the hotel room. She stripped off the trench coat and stepped into a steaming shower. She scrubbed her body without daring to look at it. She did not want the sight of her own flesh to remind her of what she had just been through.

She decided to change into the jeans and t-shirt that she had purchased at Urban Outfitters that same afternoon. Had all of this occurred in a single day? Emblazoned on the top were the words, "My boyfriend won't care because he won't know." The slogan had been prophetic. As it was so late at night and legitimately bedtime, she wore the shirt without a bra.

She returned to the concierge and asked him about the next train to Prague. It did not leave until eight a.m. As it was now midnight, she would have to wait for eight hours, the length of a workday. Well, maybe the length of a workday for most people, but not for Laura when she was employed by the advertising agency. Ten, twelve, and fourteen hour marathons had been the norm.

Her legs felt weak and she thought she might tumble to the floor. Was it because of Byron or the thought of her former job? It did not matter. They were both her exes. She wanted to lie down on the cool marble and fall into a dreamless sleep.

Knowing this was impossible, she instead asked the concierge for a map of Berlin.

"Certainly," he replied. He unfolded a map and drew a big dot on their location. "You are here. We are on the *Kurfürstendamm* in West Berlin. We have the best shopping in the Republic. And this is the Bahnhof Zoo. It is the big Underground station. You can go anywhere from here." He drew a circle around the U and then a thick line from one end of the city plan to the other. "And this is the East, where everything is happening."

It was twelve a.m. and he spoke to her as if it were high noon. Where did he think Laura was going at this hour?

"Thank you." She took the marked up map and headed over to a swanky settee.

She sat down. She could sleep right here. People might mistake her for a homeless person. Eight hours was a long time. She read the map if only to give her something to do. And then she saw it: "Memorial to the Murdered Jews of Europe." This must be it. This must be the Holocaust Memorial.

It was illustrated as a park, not an indoor facility. It might be open.

*

Back out on the *Kurfürstendamm*, her backpack slung over her shoulder, Laura spotted the U sign for the Underground. It was on an island in the middle of the street directly in front of the hotel. Why had she not noticed this before? The Memorial also was on a subway line. Laura decided to be brave and descend into the Underground after midnight.

The token booth was closed. There was a self-service ticket machine. The German instructions were inadequately lit. As she struggled to decipher them, a train appeared in the station. Laura did not want to stay alone in the tube for as long as it took her to figure out how to operate the machine. She hopped on the subway without a ticket.

Was she even headed in the right direction? Who knew? A police officer was patrolling the car and asking the passengers for their tickets. When he came to Laura, he said something in German. Laura shook her head, indicating that she did not comprehend. He responded in

English, "The fine for riding without a ticket is sixty Euros."

That's all? "I'm sorry. I don't know how to buy one."

"Instead of paying, you can spend the night in jail. If that is your preference."

As tempting as that offer was, Laura had had it with jail cells.

"I will tell you what I will do for you. You can get off the train at the next stop and buy your ticket there."

"Thank you."

For sixty Euros, she could book a room at another (admittedly one-star) hotel where she could crash for the rest of the night. She rejected this idea, having also had her fill with hotel rooms.

At the next stop, Laura studied the map of the Underground and joyfully learned that she was traveling in the right direction. This was not due to her innate navigation skills, however. The station in front of the hotel was at the end of the line and there had been no other way for her to go.

She found and followed the instructions in English. With her ticket in hand, she stood alone on the platform. Her heart pounded as she waited for the next train. If this were one a.m. in New York, Chicago, or any other big city in the Wild Wild West, she might be dead by now.

Or she might be supremely safe in her hometown. All of America—that vast continent beyond Eastern and Western Europe, past the UK and the Atlantic Ocean—was her hometown.

CHAPTER 18:
POST-TRAUMATIC SEX SYNDROME

She was on the U train, but according to her map, needed to be on the S train in order to reach the Memorial to the Murdered Jews of Europe. She was in luck. She could ride the U to the next stop and transfer to the S at the Bahnhof Zoo Station.

The "Zoo," as the locals called it, was an imposing, complicated edifice populated by winos, hookers, and young gangstas of varying Third World ethnicities. Where was Hitler's Aryan ideal? Ironically, Laura would have found the presence of a throng of similarly blonde, Teutonic men reassuring. She scanned the electric signs for the S. To her dismay, there were several S trains, the S1, the S2, the S14. Out of fear, Laura jumped on the first S train that pulled into the station and hoped for the best.

The subway bypassed the Memorial. Laura panicked. She was on the wrong S. She had better get off at the next stop, before she ended up in the far-flung outskirts of Berlin.

Outdoors and above ground, Laura breathed a sigh of relief. The U was just a few blocks away. She could take the U (or, more prudently, a cab) back to her hotel, The Kempi. There she would be safe as long as she did not run into *them*.

The Underground experience had been so unsettling that Laura had momentarily forgotten the ménage à trois (or was it a *pas de deux?*) with Zsa Zsa and Byron. As she ventured into a new and undiscovered territory, she continued to push away those painful recollections.

Night revelers overflowed from the bars and onto the streets. Hordes of people were eating and drinking at the restaurants that seemed to be open 24/7. Amber heat lamps warmed the terraces. It would be nice to sit down and relax at one of those tables, thought Laura. It would be nice to *sleep* at one of those tables. But East Berlin was percolating! There were no empty seats.

She continued her stroll. This might be okay, she thought. If everyone in this trendy neighborhood stayed up all night along with her, she might get through the post-traumatic phase of the breakup.

An orange, blue, and gold mosaic structure was aglow in spotlights. With its triple dome roofs, Laura thought it looked Turkish or Moorish.

Laura stopped a man. He was wearing black leather pants and had a blonde crew cut. "What is that building?" she asked him.

"Synagogue" was the one word answer.

She should have known for the two armed men guarding its gates. She was coming to realize that all Jewish sites in Europe required protection such as this. Maybe her father had been right. They were all potential targets of anti-Semitic attacks.

A short block from the synagogue, Laura peered down a side street and spied two more guards. These men were patrolling a Kosher restaurant. Laura could tell from the Hebrew lettering on the sign. Evidently, in Germany, enjoying a bowl of matzo ball soup was fraught with danger.

Laura loved matzo ball soup. She was willing to risk being blown to smithereens, knowing that each spoonful would conjure up memories of her lost mother and grandmother. If she succumbed to terrorists, Byron would never know. Her passport instructed that in case of emergency, call her father.

With this morose vision, Laura recognized that she was unable to envision her life beyond this moment.

It was, however, at this moment that she came upon an intriguing cluster of decaying structures. She followed the sound of loud music down a dank passageway. Behind the buildings, a bonfire illuminated the post-modern, post-Soviet, post "end-of-the-world-as-we-know-it" crowd.

Again, no empty seats, so she sat down on a boulder. In the

distance, she could make out the silhouette of a young man with blonde dreadlocks. He appeared to be staring at her, but it was hard to tell. The moonlight was fading. Soon, it would be dawn. Her ordeal would be over, or would it be just beginning?

The unusual Rastafarian man moved toward her. He had ivory skin and pale green eyes. "Is this your first time here?" His voice had the familiar twang of the Great Plains of the United States.

"It is!" Laura was amazed at how upbeat she sounded, given her distraught emotional state. "Where are you from?" She recognized in her own voice the hint of Bohemia.

"Kansas."

She was tempted to say, "You're not in Kansas anymore." It would feel good—awesome, in fact—to talk NCAA basketball with a fellow Midwesterner. Instead, in that split second, she made the decision to withhold her All-American Girl identity.

"I am from Prague," she announced deliberately and with an unequivocal Eastern European accent.

"Then it is true what they say about Czech girls."

"What is that?"

"That they are the most beautiful in the world. How long will you be in Berlin?"

"I am out of here in the morning."

Laura watched his expression. He seemed to be relishing the idea of a No Strings Attached hookup with an exotic Czech girl. In Laura's day, it was called a one-night stand. In this case, with her time constraints, it would amount to a quarter-night stand.

"Must you go so soon? I'm performing here tomorrow night with my band. It would be an honor to have you in the audience."

"You are a musician? What do you play?"

"The vibes."

Laura was genuinely confused. "What are these 'vibes'?"

"The vibraphone. Like an electronic xylophone."

"Oh. So, you play the cool jazz." She was making the effort to convey enthusiasm, but fatigue overwhelmed her. She needed to lie down and go to sleep.

"I play everything: Island, fusion, and yes, jazz. Would you like a solo performance? I can give you one in my studio."

"Where is this studio?" Laura asked. He was already helping her down from the boulder.

"Upstairs." He indicated the middle of the three ramshackle buildings. It was several stories high.

She agreed.

He led her through a tunnel and up a wide stairwell. The walls were plastered with signs protesting George Bush, the wars in Iraq and Afghanistan, American Imperialism, and Global Hegemony. Laura did not see any swastikas.

"These buildings were slated for demolition until the squatters took over. Now there are artists on every floor. They keep their studios open all night so that the tourists can buy their art. There is even a rooftop bar and movie theater. If you stayed longer, you could—"

"Is not possible," she interrupted.

He undid the padlock to his door. They entered a smallish room painted glossy white. Under the windowpane, there was a bed. To Laura, this was the most welcoming feature. She ignored everything else in the studio—the array of percussion instruments, the reggae posters—and climbed into it.

"By the way, my name is Thomas."

"I am Lara," she said, recreating her name to sound fuzzily Bohemian. "I hope I am not giving you wrong idea." She let her hair splay across the pillow and curled up her legs. "I am tired."

"No problem." The vibraphone was kitty corner in the room. Thomas got behind it and turned it on. "You can listen, go to sleep, or do whatever pleases you."

By his third suggestion, Laura thought he meant that she should remove her clothes and masturbate for him. It was not such an outrageous proposal, as Thomas's playing and the mellow chimes were soothingly seductive.

Without warning, she saw a mental picture of Zsa Zsa and Byron. It had uncontrollably appeared in her consciousness.

Panic seared through her veins. She was overtaken by the urge to run away. She recognized this as a fright and flight response. Laura was having a major anxiety attack. If she were not such a self-sufficient type, she would have fallback drugs in her backpack. All she would have to do is swallow several (or more) pills to quell her nerves.

"Thomas?"

"Yes?"

"Can you come here for a minute? I do not feel well."

"Did you have too much to drink, sweetie? Here. Let me give you some fresh air." The music stopped when he put down the mallets. He mounted the bed, standing over her with his legs straddling her body. She had a low angle view of his crotch.

As Thomas opened the window, ashes from the bonfire outside soared into the room and landed on her face. The young man, Laura duly noted, had a huge bulge in his pants. He collapsed on top of her.

What a relief it was to have his weight on her chest. She adjusted his arms and legs so that they covered her own four limbs.

"Push hard against me, Thomas."

"My pleasure," he replied, mistaking her request as sexual when it was in fact medicinal. The immense pressure and flattening of her body had the effect of wringing out from her all of the nausea and prickliness.

"I feel so much better."

"Me, too." He spoke softly as he wiped the embers from her face. Glancing down at the "boyfriend . . . won't know" message on her t-shirt, he asked, "Is there a boyfriend in Prague?"

Laura shook her head no.

He reached underneath the shirt and caressed her breasts. She wasn't wearing a bra. It was electrifying. *See?* She was not going to be miserable forever. She was not going to let *them* deprive her of the joy of sex. No sir-re.

Laura sighed. At her small capitulation, Thomas stiffened and grew urgent. She ever-so-slightly parted her lips for him. He voraciously kissed her. The spiraling movements of their tongues reminded her of twisted strudels. Relaxing all of the muscles around her head, she accepted him, fully embodying her role as Eastern European temptress.

"Sir Thomas," she moaned.

He unzipped and pulled down her tight jeans. His hand found her hole.

"Oh, baby! You're so wet."

How could that be? She barely knew Thomas. It had been no more than two or three hours since the devastation with the man she loved. Was she not suffering from post-traumatic sex syndrome? She shuddered at the creeping thought that the liquid was left over from *them*.

Thomas of course interpreted her wetness as a sign of desire for him and that she was giving him the green light. In response, he put his pedal to the metal and gunned her.

When he entered her, it hurt like hell. Her inner sanctum felt like gritty sandpaper against his camshaft. Laura began gasping like a strangled kitten. She wanted him to stop. She almost said no, but could see that he was so enthralled and into her. She knew it was not his fault. The stinging soreness was due to Zsa Zsa and Byron. They were the cause of this physical agony, which she now chose to tolerate. It was preferable to facing the abyss of loss and betrayal.

He heaved into her, coiled her hair with his hands, and groaned. Mercifully, the sex was over quickly. He seemed to want to stay right there. She shimmied free from him. Once he was out, her insides were throbbing. She bunched up the blanket and stuffed it between her legs. It felt like a diaper, especially as it was absorbing her juices, but Laura did not care. It was comforting.

"Is something wrong?"

"No. Everything is peachy."

"Did I hurt you?"

"Is okay. I will live."

"You were great. I want to make it up to you."

"You make it up to me by letting me stay here. I have no other place to go. My train leaves very soon."

"Not so fast. You can stay as long as you like. It is not every day that I have in my bed a kinky Chechnya girl. No?"

"Czech girl," she corrected him.

"Right. Don't go away."

CHAPTER 19:
KINKY CZECH GIRL MEETS SIR THOMAS MORE

"You are a kinky Czech girl, yes?"

"Perhaps," she answered into the pillow. She was lying on her stomach. Thomas sat down on the bed and tapped on her butt with the vibraphone mallets. Their pompom ends felt soft.

"I think you are," he said. Laura felt the reverse ends of the sticks tantalize her asshole. It actually felt pretty good. But she did not want him plunging anything up her ass. She had to draw the line somewhere.

"I cannot have foreign objects placed inside of my body."

"Why not?"

Why not indeed? "It is against the law in my country. We have already had too many invaders in Czechoslovakia. You know, during all the wars. I—I mean they—will not allow us to have any more."

"Am I a foreign object?"

"You are strange to me, yes, but not an object. I am completely serious about this. It is—what is the word—ignoble."

"You mean noble."

"No. I don't." She turned over to face him.

"You shaved your pussy." He proceeded to beat the percussion wands on her lower abs. "I guess there is no national prohibition against *that*."

"I did not do this," Laura said, as she covered herself with her hands.

"Who did?"

"I do not like to say."

"The boyfriend who won't care because he won't know?" He

referred to Laura's Urban Outfitters t-shirt.

"Exactly. He did it."

"I don't mind. I get to reap the benefits."

Using the blunt end of one of the vibraphone mallets, he pried open her folds. With the balled end of the other, he rhythmically rolled over her kernel. Laura suddenly thought of cornhusks and sugar. What crops did they grow in Kansas?

As if she cared. Thomas, it turned out, was a genius. That's all she knew. How could she have ever doubted the authenticity of her desire for him? There was no doubting this Thomas! She let go of the absurd claim of a Czech moratorium on sex with inanimate objects. Why the hell not? This was so amazing and Thomas was—oh! So great!

"Oh, Thomas," she moaned. "Sir Thomas, yes. Sir Thomas. More. Oh yes, more!" She was calling out the name of the Catholic saint, Sir Thomas More. So! Be! It! All she wanted was him, whoever *he* (or it) was, and the exquisite release that was his to withhold and his to grant. A violent orgasm quaked through her body, which bounced off the grungy bed sheets as if she were on a trampoline. As the convulsions eventually subsided, her screams segued into peals of laughter.

"I guess you liked that."

"Yes, Sir Thomas. I did." She wiped away tears. Tears? She *had* liked it. *Like* was an understatement, yet there were tears in her eyes. They were not of happiness. Sadness suddenly conquered her. Post-traumatic sex syndrome. It was ecstasy chased by grief. If she stayed in this bed—in this room—a second longer, she would burst out crying.

"I must go now," she said, leaping out of bed.

"So soon? Stay a while. You just came. Literally."

"I cannot do this." She sifted through the bedding in search for her clothes.

"Then it is true what they say about Czech girls."

"What?" she asked impatiently. He had already used this line on her once before. She found her jeans and was putting them on.

"That all they want is a rich American man that they can marry and leach off of. Obviously, you've got the wrong guy."

"That is not who I am." For a moment, she dropped the phony inflections. Had he confused the Prague princesses with Russian mail order brides?

"Why would you want to be with me, a struggling musician?"

"It is not that. I have been crushed by a man."

"It can be different with me. Come on . . . " He stopped in midsentence. He seemed to be mining for something meaningful to say. "I apologize. I forgot your name."

She laughed. The insult was minor, given all she had been through. Fully dressed, she grabbed her backpack and headed for the door.

In a flash, Thomas got dressed. He bounded after her, down the steps to the tunnel.

"Tell me your name!" He called after her, his voice echoing.

Whatever for?

When he caught up with Laura, he said, "You're the first gal I've had sex with—"

"Yeah, right," she interrupted, turning briefly to glance at him.

"—since I arrived in Berlin."

"I have been with many more people." She reclaimed her Bohemian accent.

"People? As in both men and women? Are you a pro?"

"Yes. No. It depends on the question." She giggled in spite of herself.

"Forgive me. That was out of line. I have much more respect for you than that. I think you are fascinating. You are lovely to look at it, but it is your inner self that is so . . . Hey, I don't know what I am saying. Look." He indicated the nearby street and early morning light. "A new day has dawned. Would you like to go somewhere and get some coffee? What do you say, Lara?"

"You know my name."

"It just came to me." He was smiling.

*

It was six a.m. Laura was exhausted. Had she slept at all in Thomas's studio? At most, there had been a fleeting catnap when Thomas had gone to get the vibe mallets. She admired his golden dreadlocks and fought an impulse to confide in him, to spill her sordid saga to a friend, but Thomas was not this person. They had just met. Besides, he believed her to be a free-spirited Czech girl, not the uptight, middle-aged American that she really was.

At this hour, everything seemed to be closed. They finally came upon a sterile establishment that was part of a chain. They ordered two cups of joe and carried them to their table. The chairs—the shape of which did not conform to the human body—wobbled as they sat down. The metal tabletop had useless round holes. Whoever designed this place seemed to be sending the message, "Don't sit here!" Or "Don't sit here for very long! This is valuable, revenue generating real estate. Eat, drink up, and get moving!"

But Laura and Thomas were the only customers and could take their sweet time, if they wanted to. As if they had any common ground and were friends. She took a sip of the coffee. It scalded her tongue. For the next day or so, she would be unable to perform fellatio. Not that it mattered. Not now. Lord Byron was no longer a part of her life.

Thomas removed the plastic lid and allowed his coffee to cool. He began, "In the States, when two people meet, the first thing they ask each other is, 'What do you do?' So, being a typically superficial American, I must ask you. Lara, what do you do?"

Good question. She decided to make up something. "I am—how do you say in English—a spokesmodel for cell phones."

"Are you famous?"

"Am I famous? Yes, of course. In my own country, I am very famous. There are billboards, magazine ads, TV commercials."

"That is quite a career."

She nodded in agreement. "I do . . . okay!"

He continued. "In America, everyone is defined by their jobs. That was one of the reasons I left. Do you understand what I am saying?"

"I think so. In Prague, it is not that way. The job is not—what is the expression—the 'end all' that it is in your country. In Prague, it is also important to be new."

"New? You mean as in new money?"

"Not only the money. New clothes, new friends, new cell phone, everything must be new. It is like Madonna, ever-changing, always reinventing oneself—"

She stopped in midsentence, before she could reveal her mastery over the English language.

"I can see that with you."

She twirled her hair and beamed at him. She was getting really good at this.

"You are my mystifying Czech girl."

She leaned forward and spoke more quietly. "For the Czech people, this is true. For others, this is not so true."

"What others?"

She pointed to her shirt.

"Ah, yes. The boyfriend who won't care."

She nodded. "He is defined by the past. His father was a Nazi and he is a neo Nazi."

"You should never have gone out with him. For me, it would be like dating a terrorist. It's un-American."

"It is worse than un-American for me."

"How so? Don't tell me he abused you."

"Sexually and emotionally. As you can see, I am no more with him."

"I am sorry, Lara. Say, I didn't do anything that reminded you of your ex, did I?"

She smiled slyly. He had (the strangeness of it) and she had liked it. "There is one more thing you can do for me."

"What is that?"

She unfolded her map of Berlin and pointed to the Memorial to the Murdered Jews of Europe. "I want to go here."

He studied the street plan and then the lines of the Berlin Underground system. "Do you see that stop?" He indicated the one right outside the window. "You can take the U one stop to the S and then the S two stops to the Memorial. Before moving to Berlin, I had never been on a subway. Not bad for a boy from Kansas."

Laura recalled her confusion in the Berlin Underground the night before. "Will you take me there, Sir Thomas?"

"Gladly. Let's go."

CHAPTER 20:

MEMORIAL TO THE MURDERED JEWS OF EUROPE

Laura and Thomas sat on a granite block at the beginning of the Memorial to the Murdered Jews of Europe. The park was an undulating field of stones that began as low, wide slabs and progressed to towering, rectangular posts. Laura was surprised to see so many tourists parading about at such an early hour and in the dreary weather.

The smooth surface on which they sat radiated warmth. It was probably from the hot sun of the previous day. Laura found this consoling and comforting. She thought that she could sleep right here, in the Holocaust Memorial. It was unlikely that she would make the eight a.m. train.

As Thomas studied her face, Laura assumed he was appraising her disheveled and ordinary appearance. What a sight she must be! She had showered a few hours ago, back at The Kempi. Her scrubbed complexion had no traces of makeup. In the light of day, she doubted that she looked very Czech and like one of "the most beautiful girls in the world." At the very least, he could see that she was no "girl."

"Lara, I know you say that you 'do okay!' I'm glad to hear that, but do you need any money?"

"No. I am fine."

"Are you sure? Do you have enough money to get back to Prague?"

"I will use my credit card. I am low on cash," she admitted.

He handed her a 20 Euro note. "Here."

"Thank you, Thomas." She accepted the note, grateful that she would not have to hunt down an ATM or negotiate the bewildering S and U trains back to The Kempi.

She leaned back on the rock and said, "I am very tired. I must rest for a few minutes." Drizzle sprayed her face. A faint ray of sun attempted to shatter the cloud covering.

Bending over her, Thomas eclipsed her view of the sky. He kissed her neck.

"On second thought, I am not so tired. I would like to see the Memorial." She sat up.

"Not yet."

"Yes yet."

She got down and left him, descending into the metaphoric cemetery. As she entered its depths, the stones over shadowed her. They were closely aligned in a grid. Strangers slipped in and out of view between the pillars, as if going from life to death, from existence to extinction. It was, Laura recognized, conceptual art. And as such, was the Memorial overly dispassionate?

The "Murdered Jews of Europe" were not anonymous figures. They were wives and husbands, sisters and brothers, mothers and fathers, children and grandchildren, grandparents, aunts and uncles, nieces and nephews, lovers and friends, cousins, colleagues, and classmates. The serenity here belied the madness of Hitler and the Nazis. Laura had seen unabashedly gruesome Holocaust exhibits in the United States. In Germany, the mere fact that the Memorial occupied a huge, unavoidable square at the center of Berlin was remarkable.

Someone tapped her shoulder. She turned and saw that it was Thomas. He had followed her.

"I am sorry," she said. "I should have said goodbye."

"Why are you running away from me?"

"I want to be alone."

"Look around you. Life is short and fragile. You shouldn't waste time being alone."

"You are right." She gazed down the long path between the

rocks. "Follow the Yellow Brick Road," she said meaninglessly.

"You sound like an American girl. I like it."

"Howdy," she continued with a twang.

That the enigmatic "Lara" could also be a straight talking cowgirl seemed to turn him on. He moved in on her and began kissing her neck. It was pointless to resist him. This was her most erogenous zone (above the belt). He pushed her against one of the posts, nuzzling and chomping on her ear and causing tremors throughout her body. It was inappropriate for the location, but Laura had broken so many taboos in the past few days. Would she ever be redeemed?

She looked beyond Thomas. Was that *Byron*? Her heart thumped painfully. He vanished behind one of the columns, casting a momentary reflection on the shiny surface. Was her mind playing tricks on her? Was the lack of sleep causing her to hallucinate?

"I just saw a ghost."

"That wouldn't surprise me, considering where we are."

With a billowing scarf and white cat-eye sunglasses, a chimerical Zsa Zsa floated past them.

"Make that two ghosts." She collapsed in Thomas's arms.

"Poor Lara," he murmured as he stroked her hair.

Her body dropped to the ground. As she wailed, she imagined her cries merging with the souls of the victims buried here. *This place is not a real graveyard*, Laura reminded herself. The hallowed ground on which the massacres occurred is elsewhere. Thomas helped her to her feet.

"Are you all right, Lara?"

"I will be. Once we leave here."

Thomas held her close to his chest as he led her away from the sepulchral scene. They reached the other side of the Memorial, where the rocks were again bench-like formations. The sun had started to shine. Young boys and girls were frolicking among the stones. To them, the Memorial to the Murdered Jews of Europe was a playground.

There they were! Sitting side by side on one of the granite blocks. Zsa Zsa was swinging her legs as if she too were a wild child. She leaned into Byron and said something to him. She was evil!

Byron jumped down from the rock and looked in her direction, finding Laura immediately. He ran toward her.

Laura saw that he had on his father's Nazi jacket. How dare he wear it here! It was contemptible. It was just as well that he had dumped her for Zsa Zsa. Who needed him? They were so over!

"I have been up all night looking for you. I went back to our hotel. They told me that you had been there and left." He appeared frantic.

"When was this? I never saw you."

"Two in the morning. They said that you went out alone, in the middle of the night! What were you thinking, Laura? Berlin can be a dangerous place. Do you want to be killed? Imagine the thoughts running through my mind."

"You say that as if you care. You could have come after me, but you chose to stay with—"

Zsa Zsa caught up with them.

"I did come after you, Laura. I couldn't find you. I looked everywhere."

Zsa Zsa smiled smugly at Laura and then ogled Thomas. "Hey, Laura. Who's the eye candy?"

"This is Thomas from Kansas. Thomas, this is Zsa Zsa," said Laura, resuming her Czech accent.

"It didn't take you long to find someone new," said Byron. "I have been sick with worry and you have been out carousing—"

"—picking up a new man *and* a new accent," interjected Zsa Zsa in her native Texan drawl.

"Holy Topeka, you must be the neo Nazi."

Zsa Zsa laughed. "Good one, Thomas. I've got one for you, Holy Romanian Empire."

"What? I am not a Nazi. Laura, did you tell this young man that I am a Nazi?"

"So what if I did? How can you wear that despicable jacket—from which you only recently tore off the swastikas—to a *Holocaust* Memorial? Have you no respect for the dead? Have you no remorse? Just because no one knows it is a Nazi jacket, that no one except for you and—"

"—and I," interrupted Zsa Zsa. She tossed her black mane.

Fuck you, thought Laura. *Fuck both of you.* She felt she could scream at them at the top of her lungs into perpetuity.

"You are right. And I am wrong." Byron removed the jacket, threw it on the ground, and stomped on it. "Is that better, *Geliebte*?"

"It is too late."

Laura grabbed Thomas's hand. Together they ran away from the Memorial, leaving behind Byron and Zsa Zsa, fleeing the tortured souls of Europe and, Laura hoped, her own.

CHAPTER 21:
A WHIFF OF FINALITY

"Who is that woman?" Laura asked from the back seat of a cab. She eyed the rapid repetition of placards, each bearing the identical photo of a blonde, middle-aged woman not much older than Laura. The posters were hung in the median of a divided boulevard in Berlin.

"That is Angela Merkel," said the driver. "She is poised to be our next chancellor."

"Really?" Laura was impressed.

"She has her opponents, but is the clear frontrunner. She is going to win."

I am wasting my life, thought Laura. One woman is about to become the leader of Germany and a de facto head of the European Union and Free World. The other (me, *moi*) is crumpled in the rear of a taxi, crushed by male rejection. I am pitiful, she concluded. At least in Chicago, I was employed and a woman of accomplishment. What have I come to?

*

Laura had missed the morning train from Berlin to Prague and was lucky to catch one at midday. She was in a daze. Minutes or hours flew by. Laura did not know which. When the train went through a darkened tunnel, she gazed at her amply lit reflection in the windowpane. Dark circles were under her eyes. Shadows streaked her uncombed hair. They were like the lowlights that she had always said no to at the beauty salon.

The train arrived at Prague station. She was so overtired, her surroundings seemed otherworldly. She felt out of time. It was how she imagined dead people felt just before leaving the planet Earth. She had not come to Eastern Europe to feel *dead*. The Art Nouveau station instantly awed and saved her. There was a quiet bustle of people in the cavernous lobby. It was good to be home if, in fact, she could call Prague her home.

She collapsed in yet another cab. The unregulated taxi service in Prague was not cheap and she was splurging on a ride to her neighborhood in Prague 2. What did it matter? She still had money. *For how much longer?* Laura wondered, as the driver pulled up to her building. Its peeling lavender paint was reassuring to her. She climbed the stairs and unlocked the door to her loft. She was back at last.

The room was warm and the windows were shut. She recognized the faint fragrance of gardenias. It was from the shampoo she had used the last time she was here. That had been such a long time ago. No, it was not. It may have felt like eons, but had been exactly six days. What a journey!

One that is over. Maybe this is for the best, she tried to tell herself. Where had she thought this relationship was going? She had dreaded telling her dad that she was romantically involved with the son of a Nazi. What if Laura and Byron had one day decided to live together or marry? She could not have continued to hide the truth from her father.

Yet her feelings for Byron were undeniable and she yearned to live her life as she saw fit. Byron made her feel beautiful, desired, cherished, and protected, as no man had ever done before.

Their attraction to each other was beyond the realm of normal physics.

Also for Laura, a former businesswoman, there was a practical consideration. In five years, she would be fifty years old. Byron was a handsome, physically fit, and mentally stimulating man *and* he was close to her age. She *liked* that he was complicated and took risks. It would be a joy to grow old with him. Meeting him may have been a gift from the universe. Would she ever find this again?

She had—quite possibly—fallen everlastingly in love in less than one week!

How long would it take Laura to recover from this breakup? Referring to her inner book of dating wisdom, compiled from years of experiences, she predicted double the amount of time of the actual relationship. Using that formula, she would be mended in twelve to fourteen *days*. Laura feared that it would take more like twelve to fourteen *years*. Before she could face the arduous healing process, she needed to get some sleep.

She stripped off all of her wrinkled clothes. She opened the window. Daylight lingered. She slid beneath the duvet cover sans the actual duvet. The sheets seemed starched with the dried up fluids of their lovemaking. Laura deeply breathed in the musky smell. When she detected the scent of Byron, she started to weep.

Tears streamed out of her, drenching her pillow, her face, and her hair. She had let another woman come between them. It was too terrible. Should she have fought harder for her man? Was he worth it? Was any man? In the combative mode, she punched the mattress with her fists and the balls of her feet.

In Bratislava, he had shared her with another man, Sergei. She had willingly participated in both threesomes (two men and one woman, two women and one man) insofar as the dynamics had favored *her*. Once Laura was no longer the center of attention, she had reacted like a jejune girl.

Or had she? Was she trying to justify his behavior? She turned over the pillow and rested her cheek on the dry side. In the back of her mind, there was a hidden truth. If only she could find it. She was blinded by his final deed, repeated ad infinitum in the Room of Mirrors. As she replayed those few seconds, Laura felt jealousy, anger, and (admittedly) a twinge of sexual arousal. Above all, she experienced the horrible pain of losing him. There was an empty aching at the depths of her soul. She burst out crying again.

She was lolling in a swamp of tears. Her sinuses were engorged. She got up from the bed and went into the bathroom. She blew her nose into a bath towel. (It was more efficient than a box of tissues.) What a relief. A familiar siren pealed outside. A fire truck clattered on her street below. The high-pitched sound was not unlike . . .

Laura remembered the shrill alarm that had gone off when she was fleeing the Apocalypse Hotel. Had he come after her? He had said that he had. The loud piercing noise may have covered up the calling out of her name.

She replaced the towel on the rack. In so doing, she wondered what might have been had they never left the fair city of Prague. Tonight she might be using this very towel to wipe up his semen. What a wonderfully wretched thought! It would bring her complete bliss.

She returned despondently to the creased and tangled bedding on the floor. It bore stripes of streetlights and the gloom of evening. In spite of her new insight, it was over. Pallid, guileless Laura had allowed herself to be trumped by the dark and conniving Zsa Zsa. He was lost to her forever. Her frame convulsed with sobs before she finally fell into a deep sleep.

CHAPTER 22:
THE SUN ALWAYS RISES

The next morning, Laura awoke rested and refreshed. She had slept for eleven hours. She showered and began to dress as if it were any other day, B. B. E., "Before the Byron Era." The question with which Laura grappled was how could she resort to her prior life after everything she had been through? Their romance had changed her forever.

What to wear in the A.D., "After the Debacle"? Most of her clothes were dirty. Her wardrobe included one ensemble that she had not yet worn in Prague. It consisted of a black gossamer dress. She had purchased it at the end of 1993 when Heroin Chic had been all the rage. Her decision to bring it meant also packing a pair of hefty combat boots. Not to mention the requisite black lipstick.

When Laura slipped on the dress, she was pleased by how it fell on her gaunt figure. She was the perfect mannequin for the anorexic, debauch style.

She headed out to the Globe Café. It was a brave move. It was there that she had met Byron. On that day, the customers had been seeking refuge from the rain and it was afternoon teatime. Today, the sun shone brightly and people were eating breakfast. Breakfast? What was that? Laura had slept through the morning rush since relocating to Eastern Europe.

Maybe this will be the start of a new routine, her inner clock finally in sync with the locals.

Laura glanced over at the young woman seated at the next table. Her shiny brown hair was immaculately swept back from her face and held in place by jeweled combs. Under the track lighting, her powdered forehead sparkled.

I am dreary by comparison, thought Laura. *Face it—you mean old*. At the height of Heroin Chic, the younger woman was in elementary school. What had possessed Laura to leave the house in this Gothic get-up? The answer was obvious. She was in mourning.

The girl was intensely drawing on a large sketchpad. Are those storyboards? Laura wondered. She was applying a multitude of colored chalks to create lifelike figures in a series of squares. Storyboards were done during the preproduction phase for films and commercials. Laura had used them at the ad agency.

Laura guessed it was a comic book. That was what the young artists worked on nowadays. *I hope not. When I was that age, I was overflowing with traditional ambition.*

Whatever her purpose, the girl was fully engaged in a project. This was more than could be said about Laura. What would be her next step? She had no clue. She feared that she would spend the rest of her days in a morose state. She would turn into a crazed, anachronistically dressed woman, wandering the streets of Prague. Was this her unavoidable fate? She would not let this happen to her.

Okay! She would do what she had always done when faced with a seemingly insurmountable challenge. She would make a list, known in corporate parlance as a strategic plan. When written in the wake of a major blow, it provided solutions as to how to recoup revenue.

Laura needed her computer. She was used to documenting her goals and progress on an Excel spreadsheet. You are not at work, she reminded herself. You just broke up with your boyfriend. What you need is a blueprint for adventure and fun.

At minimum, she needed something with which to write. She turned to the girl next to her, hoping she understood English. "Do you have a pen?"

The girl gazed up from her drawing. A wave of recognition seemed to cross her face. She stared at Laura. "I think so. Let me check."

She rummaged through a leather tote. Its soft material reminded Laura of the messenger bag Byron had been carrying on the day they had met at a nearby table. Laura felt an irrational pang of exclusion, brought about by the commonality of the two bags. This satchel had short handles, whereas Byron's had a long shoulder strap.

"Here, I found one." The girl held up a pen in a victorious gesture. She handed it to Laura.

"Thank you!"

She considered asking the young woman for an empty page from her drawing pad, but decided against it. The parchment looked expensive. That and it would be a daunting task to fill up an 11 by 17 piece of paper!

A beverage napkin would have to do. On it, she wrote the number one. Around it, she drew a circle. What would top her list of next escapades? Her mind drew a blank.

Don't think about it. Just write. She wrote the words, "Find a job." The eight characters blotted in blue ink were shocking. They had materialized from the recesses of her brain. Now that they had, they made sense. A job would give Laura a much-needed focus. There was only one major hurdle. She spoke almost no Czech, which seriously limited her employment prospects.

Number two, in another circle. She wrote, "Find a new boyfriend." *Oy vey*, thought Laura. Had she no imagination? That was all she needed. If she must she must, but her one criterion for a new lover would be that he spoke no English. An affair with a sexy non-communicative (save for the grunting) foreigner might be the perfect antidote for her broken heart.

I am not really getting anywhere with this list, she thought.

Number three. The exercise was exhausting her. Job, love life. What else was there? "Call Dad," she wrote, underlining the words. They had not spoken in over a week. She should call him right now. Laura hesitated because her father knew her so well. He would be able to tell that something was wrong. He might insist that she come home. She did not want him to worry. She vowed to call him very soon.

She turned over the napkin.

"You can have your pen back. Thank you for lending it to me."

"No problem. By the way, I *love* your dress."

"This?"

"Yes. When you sat down, I thought only a Czech model could pull that off at ten in the morning."

"I am way too old to be a model." And too short, she mentally added.

"You could be a former model."

"No. And I'm not Czech either."

"Neither am I, obviously. My boyfriend is. Where are you from?"

"Chicago."

"I don't believe it! So am I!"

"Wow! That's amazing. What are you doing here?"

"I'm living with my boyfriend, Leo. We met at the Art Institute of Chicago and then he got accepted to the Prague film school. I decided to come with him."

"What are you working on? I was admiring your pastel drawings. They're fabulous." Laura meant it.

"Thanks! They're sketches for Leo's film. Here. Check these out." She flipped the pages to drawings of the Prague Castle in increasing stages of destruction. "He's a maniac, isn't he? He's going to blow up the Prague Castle."

"Don't say that too loud! People will think we're terrorists."

The young woman laughed. "Don't worry. It's only a movie. He's doing it with models and special effects."

"Very cool."

"What are you doing here? Are you on vacation?"

"A very long vacation." She wanted to tell her everything. She yearned to cry out, "I just broke up with my boyfriend! It happened yesterday!" It was universal girl melodrama. She said instead, "My name's Laura. It's very nice to meet you."

"I'm Jolene. It's great meeting you, too."

Laura thought Jolene looked familiar. Where had she seen her before? Prague or Chicago?

Laura asked, "Do you have other work in Prague? Other drawings that you did for school or for yourself?"

"I do. Lots. I have a studio in our apartment. And I do commercial work for the ballet company here."

"The ballet company? I've seen your work! On a poster tacked to a street pole."

"Oh my gosh, that *was* you. I thought it might be. It was early in the morning—"

"I remember! I was so embarrassed. My clothes and my hair. I was a mess."

"No, no. *You* looked great. *I* was the one taking out the trash."

They giggled.

"Your work is really good," said Laura.

"Thank you."

"Are you looking for representation? Because if you are, I know of a dealer who is very committed to promoting the work of young artists such as yourself. I can put you in touch with him. Would you be interested?"

"Yes, I would love that!"

A silver crucifix hung from Jolene's neck. Laura was unaccustomed to seeing someone in Eastern Europe wearing religious jewelry. It made her like the woman even more than before.

"Can I borrow your pen again?"

"Sure."

On the back of a napkin, Laura jotted the name and cell phone number of the one art dealer she knew in all of Europe. She handed the napkin to Jolene.

"Byron Baumgaarten," Jolene read.

The sound of his name made Laura's heart leap.

"Thank you *so* much."

"Good luck. I hope it works out."

During her interaction with Jolene, Laura's mood had improved tremendously. By performing this small act of kindness, it felt like Byron was back in her life. He *isn't*, Laura reminded herself.

Inasmuch as Laura wanted to be friends with Jolene, she decided (regrettably) not to give out her own contact information. It would be too tempting to ask how things were going with Byron and devastating if Zsa Zsa came up in the conversation.

"I'm glad we met," Laura said as she got up to leave.

"Same here. Have a nice day."

"You, too. Have a nice day!"

As she made her way through the maze of crowded tables, eyeing the exit, Laura began to panic. Now what? She would tragically spend the rest of this beautiful day—if not all of her days—alone.

"Laura! Wait!" It was Jolene. Laura turned around. Jolene was waving the napkin with Byron's name and number on it and, Laura realized, her *list*.

"If you need a job, *I* can help *you*."

CHAPTER 23:
INTERNATIONAL MEDIA SALES

The next day, Laura was interviewing for a job. She was in a former Soviet bureaucratic center. The cinderblock walls were coated in stark white, high-gloss paint. Sleek chrome dividers broke up the rambling floor space.

Next week, these cubicles will be filled with people, the interviewer told her. He planned on hiring hundreds of salespeople for his new global enterprise, starting with this location in Prague. Very soon, he would be opening additional offices throughout Eastern Europe and beyond.

Yes, he needed English-speaking employees. Other languages were beneficial, but not required. What about Czech? Not necessary. Most business was to be conducted outside of the Czech Republic, via web phones and "the like." Laura wanted to know exactly what she would be doing. International media sales, he said.

"Can you be more specific?"

"You will sell messages on signs. Have you been to Times Square?"

"Yes." Laura restrained the impulse to roll her eyes.

"This was with the drunken party animals on New Year's Eve?"

"No. I used to go to New York City for my job. I am very familiar with the advertising in Times Square. I helped create it. And buy it. Those were my accounts—"

"Then you know the quality of my product. It is first class. I have signs like the ones you see in Times Square and in major venues all over the world. Or will have them before long. This is your chance to get in on the ground floor."

"The ground floor? Are you serious? If you look at my resume, you will see that with my advertising experience, I should be starting at the top."

"I beg to differ, Miss—?"

"—Levine. I can help you run this office while you are busy opening the others. You will not have the stress of worrying about what is going on in Prague. I can be a tremendous asset. I can give you the freedom to build your empire."

"That is out of the question."

"Why?"

He did not respond immediately. His masculinity seemed to infuse every inch of the room. His Balkan eyes were broadly set and his blatantly asymmetric face was creased and lived in. Laura recalled an NBA coach, also with a Slavic surname. Years ago, as a player, his face had been bashed during a basketball game. Laura had always found him incredibly sexy (possibly due to the major reconstructive surgery that had followed). Her potential employer was having the same effect on her. It made her uncomfortable. He was reluctant to put her in charge and Laura sensed that it was because he was a misogynist.

"I must first find out if you can sell my products. You will learn how to do things my way before you become a boss, as I am." He laughed. "You can never be—as I am—a man."

"You are absolutely right about that." Laura batted her eyelashes at him. "Yet wrong about my abilities. I am sure that I will learn everything I need to know about your products in the first few hours. If, of course, you hire me." He would be lucky to get her.

"Good. Then I will see you on Monday at nine."

"Deal." She replied with more conviction than she felt. She held out her hand for him to shake. He ignored it and gave her his business card. His first name was Damjan. Damn him, she thought.

*

Damn him, she again thought while crossing the noisy street at midday. What was she getting herself into? She had not left Chicago in order to go to work for another arrogant male. I will never go back there. That was the last time I will ever see him. She crumpled the business card and tossed it in the trash.

Nevertheless, on Monday morning, Laura found herself awaking early and getting ready for work. She showered, washed her hair, and went straight to the eighteenth century armoire.

She surveyed the rack of skimpy and frilly designer dresses. There was not a business suit in sight. Laura had intentionally not packed any.

She was determined to show her new boss that she was VP material. Maybe this will do, Laura thought as she considered the most conservative item in her wardrobe. It was a pastel seersucker dress.

She stepped into it. She zipped up the back as far as the zipper would go, which was to below her waistline. She was not showing off any cleavage, but her back was entirely bare. She had never worn this particular dress to work. Not even during the dog days of summer.

Laura possessed a deeply ingrained, dress-for-success ethic. Was this even relevant in the new world order? The young female ad execs at the agency wore flip-flops to work, the rubber soles making squish-squish noises up and down the halls of corporate America. To Laura, it was a major breach of decorum. Astoundingly, their casualness had no negative impact on their careers.

In deference to the *old* world order, Laura arranged her damp hair so that it covered most of her back. She rushed out the door, not wanting to be late for work, yet plagued by the notion that her attire was inappropriate.

As she raced down the street to catch the tram, Laura heard inside her head the Bangles singing "Manic Monday." The song had been at the top of the pop music charts in 1986, when Laura had just landed her first advertising job, the entry-level position of account coordinator.

Laura recalled the song's lyrics, which compared the manic

rush of Monday morning with Sunday and a night spent with one's lover. Unlike the goings on in the song, her Sunday had been a depiction in loneliness. Laura had drifted from one minor museum to another, staring at portraits of aristocrats from the twelfth through the seventeenth centuries, in search of a human connection. The method occasionally backfired. More than once or twice, a mid-millennium painting of a Czech duke or duchess had reminded Laura of Byron or Zsa Zsa. There was no escaping those two. Manic as it might be, Monday was a welcome relief.

She hopped on the tram, her heart beating from running to catch it. She was glad that her life was finally regaining structure.

She arrived at her new office fifteen minutes early, at 8:45 a.m. But Damjan, her boss, had beat her there.

"Well. Well. I did not expect you to show up. I thought this job was not good enough for you," was his greeting, although he was smiling at her.

"It feels great to be at work."

He raised an eyebrow, as if assessing the Americanism of what she had just said. He seemed to be contemplating two warring misconceptions, one of a lazy welfare society, the other a culture of workaholics. *Both skew the reality of my country,* she wanted to tell him. Many slog away at two full-time jobs in order to pay the bills.

Damjan brushed his stubby, angular fingers through his clumpy, brown hair. Laura spotted a bulging joint in his pinky, an early sign of arthritis. His hair had several silver strands.

He was decked out in black leather pants. His impressive physique seemed bolted to the floor. He wore black work boots, fit for urban warfare. They were speckled with plaster and white paint, evidence that he himself had done the office remodeling. An invisible field of tobacco smoke enshrouded him. It was an odor that Laura generally despised. Yet today she relished the smell, which she interpreted as a sign of his manliness.

He led her to her new workspace, one of the many vacant

cubicles. Having had her own private office for the past decade or more, Laura flinched. She was clearly starting on the bottom rung of Damjan's ladder.

"Your computer has the mobile phone numbers of potential buyers. It is fully integrated so you do not need to dial. It also has the ISP addresses of their computers for instant messaging and if you like, video. And with your looks—"

"We can do video?"

"Yes. No e-mail, I don't believe in it, remember that."

"I agree. E-mail is impersonal and can be deleted." It also leaves a trail, she thought.

"Let's try it," he said, giving her a headset.

She put it on. Reaching over her shoulder to start up her computer, Damjan grazed her naked upper back. The flickering across her skin sent shivers down her spine. The text of a sales script flashed on the screen.

"Be sure to follow the pitch word for word. It is loaded with hot buttons," he stated.

He was pressing all of her hot buttons as well. The sound of dialing filtered through the earpiece.

Damjan told her, "You're calling Tokyo. They won't be there. They've all begun their grueling commutes home. Your day is beginning and theirs is already done."

Her call went to Japanese voice mail. Again, he reached over her, disconnecting the call.

"Where will I be calling today?"

"You are a lucky girl. I have carved out for you a receptive territory: Italy, Hungary, Romania, Austria, and Slovenia."

All nations aligned with Hitler during the Second World War, thought Laura, with the possible exception of Slovenia. She was not familiar with that country. "Where is Slovenia?" she asked.

"You don't know? Slovenia is my homeland. It was once a part of Yugoslavia."

"Right. I'm sorry."

He continued, "Most Americans know of Slovenia only through their guidebooks, confusing it with Slovakia. Your movie—*Hostel* it is called—where youth are gruesomely murdered in a Slovakian hideaway, could never have taken place in my country."

He was talking about a slasher flick. "*Hostel* was made up. It was fiction. You know that, right?"

"Don't be so sure."

Damjan's words "could never have taken place in my country" echoed what Josef had said about Germans not accepting concentration camps in their own backyards, or some such myth to be imparted for generations.

Before Laura could further respond, Jolene—with her black leather tote slung over one shoulder—sashayed over to the adjacent cubicle.

"Hey, Laura. You decided to take the job. That's great."

"Thanks for telling me about it."

"No problem." She put on her headset.

Damjan placed his hands on Laura's shoulders. His touch was warm. She could feel his rough calluses. She could easily imagine what those hands could do to her. Without warning, she was besotted. It went beyond physical attraction. It was spontaneous combustion.

He said, "Jolene, you know some Spanish, yes?"

"Yes."

"You will call Spain and Portugal."

"My Portuguese is a little rusty," Jolene admitted.

"Don't worry about it. Jolene, show Laura the ropes. I will be back soon." His hands lingered on Laura's shoulders before he walked away.

When he was out of an earshot, Laura said, "I don't know these languages. Do you?"

"Not a one."

"How are we going to sell anything?"

"Everybody we call understands English. The text is peppered with one or two foreign words, in the native tongue of the person you're calling, to warm up your audience, so to speak. Not to change the subject, Laura, but did you call your father?"

"Huh? My dad? Oh, my gosh, no."

"You really should call him."

"How do you know?"

Jolene smiled mischievously.

"My list!"

"I still have the napkin. If it works out with the art dealer, I'm going to have that napkin framed. Hey, just think Laura, now you have a job, you can call your dad tonight. And tomorrow, who knows? Maybe number two on your list will come true."

"A new boyfriend?" Laura sighed in exasperation. In spite of her instant lusting over Damjan, she was not optimistic. "I don't think so."

Jolene grinned and tilted her head in the direction of Damjan's office.

"No," Laura said, feeling herself blush.

"Why not? Because he's our boss?"

"No," she repeated emphatically. She was starting to sweat.

For her part, Jolene did not say anything else about contacting Byron. While Laura was curious, it was too risky to ask. Her new friend might tell her something that was unintentionally upsetting.

Laura got to work. She was selling signs to be displayed in late July at "Musa-Fest," the Lollapalooza of Budapest. Some 400,000 young people with an annual Effective Buying Power—EBP for short—of 7.5 billion Eurodollars were expected to turn out for the weeklong event. The buzzwords were second nature to Laura. (Simple math did imply that the per-person income was quite low. It was due to the target buyers being predominantly students.) The concertgoers possessed fortunes far greater than the aggregate national products of ten Third World countries, according to the sales script.

Omitted from the pitch were the names of those ten most impoverished nations on Earth. No reason to depress your clients with abject reality. Besides, there wasn't enough time! The youthful, spend-giddy mass assembly was ready, willing, and able to buy running shoes, cell phones, iPods, digital cameras, Smartcars, designer water, beer, beer, and more beer . . . in short, whatever the client happened to be selling.

Embellishing the prepared text (if that were possible), Laura described the high-tech billboards as "omni-visible! They can be seen from everywhere!" and "omni-potent! Your sales numbers will go *way up!*" By mid-morning, Laura had received verbal commitments for 10,000 Eurodollars worth of sales.

Jolene was impressed. "You're really good at this. You don't need the teleprompter."

"Thanks. I worked in advertising in the United States."

Damjan cleared his throat. He had snuck up from behind them.

"Jolene, show Laura how to do the paperwork for the sales she has made. We need the signed contracts and authorizations for the bank transfers."

Laura looked up at him. "How am I doing?" She smiled sweetly.

She could feel the heat radiating from his body. She longed for him to separate her hair with his fingers and run his hands down her bare back. Reach into the bottom half of her dress and in so doing, bust apart the zipper. With his open palms, scoop her up by the ass and lift her from the chair. Throw her on the floor and fuck her harder, harder, yes, harder!

"I am not done with you," replied Damjan.

Laura could not believe her ears. Had he read her mind? How he must desire her, too!

"You need more training."

CHAPTER 24:
THE SLOVENIAN BEAST

Laura bounded up the steps to her Prague apartment building. She had raked in 25,000 Eurodollars in sales on her first day on the job. At the agreed-upon commission rate of 5 percent, Laura had earned 1,250 Euros for eight hours of work. It was incredible money. Annualized, it was the equivalent of 400,000 U.S. Dollars per year. At her former company, she would have had to have been on the board of directors to have made that much. She thought briefly of that time. The real gratification of occupying a seat of power would have been not the money, but the authority to give orders—and the boot—to her sociopathic ex boss (who was still there, running the agency, as far as she knew).

That period of Laura's life was over.

As Damjan had instructed, she faxed the contracts to her accounts. Mostly all were signed by the close of business. There was the small matter of the bank transfers. She was not to be paid until the clients prepaid for their advertising on the signs.

And then there was the much larger matter, the miracle of Damjan. It had been just one week since her traumatic breakup with Byron. She had feared that it would take years (at minimum two weeks) to self-mend. Laura marveled that she was way ahead of schedule for a full recovery. There was nothing like a hot new flame to snuff out the passionate fires for an old boyfriend.

Laura quickly changed into jeans and sneakers and rushed back out the door. She headed over to the Prague Zara where she purchased two moderately priced, svelte suits, both in business black.

Later that night, she put fresh sheets on her bed. She stared up at the swirling stars and imagined a new constellation, the

Slovenian Beast. It had the head of Damjan and burly arms that reached down from the sky and molested her. Involuntarily, she reached for her vulva and climaxed in less than one minute.

That makes me the One Minute Masturbator, Laura silently quipped. Like *The One Minute Manager*, a popular book and business credo from ages ago. In more ways than one, I am back in business, she thought. She smiled to herself peacefully before drifting off to sleep.

*

"Laura!" Damjan was shouting the next day. Her name rumbled through the office. His voice was a deep growl. "Please see me immediately!" She jumped in anticipation, though at the moment he sounded more angry than enamored with her. As she had on her lace-up stiletto sandals, she nearly fell on the gleaming floor. Her decision to wear these shoes was driven by an attempt to sex up her business attire. As it was, the streamlined skirt stopped at mid-thigh. The jacket had a cinched in waist that accentuated her figure. It was low cut in the front with a single button. Under it, Laura wore a sheer pink camisole.

Damjan was holding open the door to his office. After she sat down, he took his place behind his desk. He remained standing. He had on a blinding white shirt that seemed to holler, "I'm one of the good guys!" The top three buttons were undone, revealing his chest hair.

"What are these?" He was holding a stack of papers above his desk.

"Are those my contracts?"

"They are nothing." Damjan released the pages, causing them to flutter every which way on his desk and chair and the floor. "Nothing without the bank transfers. We cannot proceed without them."

"I'll get them today."

"Money, Laura, money. These are not sales without the money. Go get it."

"I will."

Had he not heard of credit? Surely, some of the advertisers could be billed. Laura did not openly question his mandatory prepay policy. Her commission would be based on a percentage of what she collected, the cold hard cash. Damjan was paying her under the table. She would report the income to the IRS when she returned to the United States.

Under the table, over the table, or, preferably, *on* the table . . . it did not matter as long as he took her down some place, sometime soon.

By Friday, Laura had made many more sales and secured the transfer of 100,000 Euros from the advertisers to the Western Union office in Prague.

Her commission earnings in her first week totaled 5,000 Euros. That was more than 6,000 USD. She had worked hard, but not *that* hard. Laura briefly wondered if everything was on the up and up. No e-mail? Western Union versus a commercial bank account? Maybe business was conducted differently in Eastern Europe than in the States. Still . . .

It was the late afternoon. A metal screen veiled the large office window. Golden sunlight filtered through.

"Yeah, yeah, yeah, I remember. Party in Prague 7," Jolene said into her cell phone. "I got it. Love you, too. Ciao." She grabbed her tote and prepared to head out.

"Have a nice weekend, Laura."

"Thanks. You, too, Jolene," she sighed.

Jolene stopped. "Say, Laura, if you're not busy, maybe you would like to come to this party. Leo's friends will be there and all they ever talk about—even after six Pilsners—is filmmaking mumbo jumbo. It's so frigging boring, you would not believe. Anyway, I'd love for you to come."

Laura was not sure. She was emotionally drained. Since Tuesday, Damjan had spoken to her less and less. It was never in private and always about the bank transfers. Finally, she had come through. It had been hard work and for what? It was obvious that he viewed her as his employee—an instrument to amass his great fortune—and nothing more.

Additionally, she would be the one "retrogressive female" (read: old broad) among a gathering of hipper and hotter than thou youngsters. She doubted her ego in its current beaten state could withstand this. Nonetheless, she replied to Jolene, "I think I will come with you. It sounds like fun."

"Great. The art dealer might be there."

Laura's heart skipped a beat. "Byron? Is he in Prague?"

"He was in Berlin when I called him. He should be back by now."

With or without Zsa Zsa? She refrained from asking. "Will he be at the party?"

"I don't know. I hope so. I told him about it. He's supposed to look at my drawings . . . *if* he shows up."

"Loob-lee-anya," Damjan was singing. "Loob-lee-anya." He had a habit of coming up from behind and startling them. "If who shows up?"

Both girls shrugged and muttered, "No one."

"I am going tonight to Ljubljana. It is a lonely ride. Laura, would you like to come with me?"

As the week had worn on, Laura had retreated each evening to her apartment, dejectedly studying the chapter on Slovenia in her guidebook. Clearly, she was devolving into a lovelorn case. For whom was she pining? That was not so clear. What she did know was this: A) Ljubljana was the capital of Slovenia; B) Damjan now wanted to scoot her off to his homeland; and C) If she saw Byron with Zsa Zsa at the party in Prague, it would kill her.

"Ljubljana. It means love in Slovene," added Damjan.

"Ooh la la," said Jolene. "I think you should go. There will be other parties in Prague, believe me."

"Sure. I am delighted to go with you, Damjan."

CHAPTER 25:
ROAD TRIP

Damjan drove a Mitsubishi Outlander. It was an SUV adapted for the tight winding streets of Eastern European villages. Its size was diminutive compared to its gas guzzling U.S. counterparts. He had the back filled to capacity with aluminum luggage. What was inside those hard cases? Evidently, he did not believe in traveling light. This was supposed to be a weekend jaunt. Or was it?

It was 600 kilometers from Prague to Ljubljana. He gave Laura a road map to look at. They were traveling south through Austria. Their route severed that country in two.

She had a new name for him: Speed Damjan. They were going fast. Laura had no idea as to how fast, because she did not know how to convert from kilometers to miles per hour. Nothing slowed him down. He owned the road. Whenever there was a car in the left lane, he revved up to it. Laura gasped. He tailgated any and all obstructions, forcing each automobile into the right lane and out of his way.

What was she doing here? It suddenly occurred to her that her options for the weekend had not been limited to two opposing men. For instance, at five p.m., she could have boarded a train to Budapest, arriving in time for singles night at the Turkish baths.

After they crossed the border into Austria, he took out a wad of cash and handed it to her. "Here are your commissions, all 5,000 Euros."

"Thanks."

"It's all there."

"I believe you." Laura folded in half the fifty 100 Euro bills. She safely tucked them in the inner pocket of her purse, zipping it shut.

"You're good, Laura."

"Thanks. What's next?"

"A pleasure holiday with your boss."

"Are you taking me to Ljubljana to show me your new office there? I can run Prague, you know."

He yanked the steering wheel and veered off the paved road. Her body jolted as they came to a screeching stop. She screamed. The SUV teetered aside a gulley.

"You know nothing, remember that. If anyone asks you why you are with me in Ljubljana, you say that you are a tourist and my guest. You got that?"

Was he crazy? "Isn't that what we're doing?"

"I thought you were a smart American girl and knew better." He shifted into reverse. The four wheels crunched pebbles and drew up dirt. He hit the gas pedal again and resumed driving.

She had known better. Her instinct—in fact, all logic—had told her that his business was a scam. There had been red flags, only she had chosen to ignore them. Her infatuation with Damjan and dazed mental state throughout the week had gotten the better of her.

One hundred thousand Euro notes (minus her cut, the five grand) were likely stashed in the back of the Outlander. He had no intention of honoring the advertising buys and putting up the signs. They were crossing international borders as felons.

"Is there a mall in Ljubljana?"

"Don't be silly. We aren't going shopping. We are taking the cash to the cleaners. Isn't that what you say in your country?"

"In B movies," Laura mumbled.

"What?"

"It's called money laundering."

Laura had never stolen anything in her life. Knowingly going along with Damjan made her an accomplice in these crimes. The only solution was to go to the police and turn him in. With her knowledge of the operation, she would see that all of the monies were returned to the appropriate clients.

Laura decided to change the subject. "Will I meet your family?"

"No. Everyone is dead."

"I am so sorry." Laura thought of her mother. She was grateful that she had her father. Her father: She still had not called him. The clash between her recent waywardness with a Nazi heir and the good daughter he knew and loved was unsettling. Yet her affair with Byron was nothing compared to her latest foray into grand larceny. Now more than ever, she was really giving her dad a reason to worry.

"I am an orphan. I am fifty years old and I call myself that. It has been for some time. My parents were political prisoners. The Soviets tortured and murdered them."

"That is terrible."

"You don't have to tell me. The Russians, the Serbs, the Germans, everywhere it is the same. The world is a violent, inhumane place."

"The Germans?"

"The Germans are the worst. Their Hapsburg Dynasty controlled Slovenia for more than five centuries and sent thousands of Slovenes to be slaughtered on the battlefields of World War I."

"I'm Jewish."

"I rest my case. Know your enemies."

"My grandfather fought in World War I."

"On what side?"

"The United States, of course. He emigrated in order to avoid going into the Russian Army, which was brutal for the Jews. Once he landed on American soil, he joined the U.S. Army, turned around, and went back to Europe. He fought in France."

"Your grandfather sounds like my kind of guy," Damjan said with sincerity.

"He was a great patriot. My relatives left the old country at the turn of the last century. They were poor. There was nothing to keep them in Europe."

"Your family was lucky. They missed Hitler."

She thought of the Jewish intelligentsia and business class that had stayed in Germany, only to be stripped of their rights, dignity, property, and lives.

"I know." She said blithely, "It pays to have peasant ancestors."

Had her heritage been different—had she grown up in a household of Holocaust survivors—her involvement with Byron would have been unthinkable.

"You do not know true suffering, Laura love lily."

"I agree. What did you call me?"

"Laura love lily." He smiled, looking away from the road and at her.

"You have a new name for me," she said.

"Yes. It suits you in your lily white dress." He turned his eyes back on the highway.

"I have a new name for you, too."

"You do?" His mood was uncharacteristically cheerful. "What is it?"

"Speed Damjan."

He laughed heartily. "I like it."

She felt herself caving in to him. It was dangerous. She reminded herself that he was a thief, but their conversation had brought tears to her eyes.

Laura gazed out the window to her right, where the sun had set about a half an hour ago. Far beyond, across more land and the Atlantic Ocean, was America, her home.

*

The digital clock read 22:00, meaning that it was ten p.m., the start time of the party in Prague. They reached the border of Slovenia. Damjan displayed both their passports. Laura was nervous. It was logical that the patrol officer would want to inspect the luggage stockpiled in the back of the Outlander. She hoped Damjan could sweet talk them in Slovene.

The guard pointed his flashlight at Laura, illuminating her

dress. Its pure whiteness was well suited for a wedding—in this case, an elopement of sorts—and the see-through fabric perfect for the honeymoon afterwards.

"He wants to see your backpack. Show it to him."

She easily gave it up. Her backpack was the least of her concerns. She feared that the official would open the hard metal cases in the back. Or worse, her purse, with the Euros inside. Then, they both would be doomed.

He inspected the bag. A beam of light danced inside the knapsack, creating orbs of iridescent pink. The guard tossed the bag back to Damjan. He again aimed the searchlight at her dress.

He uttered something in Slovene and waved them on. Laura exhaled.

"What did he say?"

"He complimented me on my beautiful whore."

The sky was a starless, moonless black. There were mountain ranges on either side. As they rode in silence, Laura found the wilderness creepy.

She began, "I can do something to make the trip go by more quickly."

"Like what? We will be there in an hour. I thought I was driving fast enough for you."

Inexplicably, Laura wanted to give him a blow job. She searched her mind for an explanation. The longing for closeness, boredom induced by the tedious road trip, her sense of adventure (hey, why not!) were all possibilities. None truly seemed to justify her urge.

Perhaps she wanted to re-enact the blow job she had given Byron on the train. In the car, with Damjan driving, she imagined chomping on his dick, causing them to swerve off the road. Then, she would jump out of the Outlander and flag down the police.

There it was. A rational explanation for her irrational desire.

Where were the highway cops? They were conspicuously absent from the roadway.

"You are driving fast enough for me. That is why I call you Speed Damjan."

"Then what is your problem?"

"My problem is that I like you a lot and you barely notice me."

"I notice you."

"You ignored me all week. You notice me only when it is financially expedient for you to do so."

"Trust me. I notice you all the time."

"You do?"

"Yes. You are hard to ignore."

"You don't know what kind of girl I am."

"A typically shallow American girl, wouldn't you say?"

Better not dignify that comment with a verbal comeback. Instead, she moved closer to him and slipped her hand between his thighs. He kept a steely gaze on the road. Laura plopped her head down on his lap, her blonde ringlets forming a mop. She pictured Damjan immersing her curly top in a bucket of soapy water and wringing her out. He continued to drive without regarding her.

Like a cheetah, she went after him, unbuckling his belt, unzipping his pants, and unbuttoning his shirt. She pulled down his briefs and exposed his thick black hair. The density invoked for Laura a fairy tale setting, where gnarly trees might at any time morph into goblins. Rising from this forest, Damjan's impressive dong was King.

So much for not noticing her!

She clutched it and brought it up to her lips, experiencing the shock of the new. It was jarringly not her buddy, the affable Lord Byron. Moreover, this banana had skin—foreskin! Meaning one thing, that Byron had been circumcised!

How had she not noticed that?

Byron's mother and father had had their infant son circumcised. Why? Out of reverence for the Jewish covenant? Had the ritual been performed (as commanded) when Byron was eight days old?

Before a houseful of guests by a *mohel* in the Jewish ceremony known as a *bris*?

Extremely doubtful. Nonetheless, many years after the procedure, Laura derived great comfort from being close to Byron. So much so, that it took another man's foreignness to jolt her into awareness.

Unsure of what to do with the strange skin, she rolled it back. Damjan was teeming with sexual energy. When was the last time he had been with a woman? Not long ago, probably. Despite his erratic and obnoxious personality, Laura assumed that he effortlessly conquered most female prey. For the past five days, she had been swooning over him nonstop.

Finally, Damjan let out a moan. "Oh! What are you doing to me? Do you want to kill us both?" He yanked up her dress and stuck his finger into her hole.

"Ouch!" Her voice was stifled in the limited space between his crotch and the steering wheel. She could no longer see a thing.

Whose idea was this anyway? It had been *her* idea and it was a *bad* idea. They might crash!

Using both hands, he grabbed her head and forced her mouth up and down along his shaft. Logical Laura asked herself, What third hand is guiding the car? As his thighs squeezed her, she realized how he was steering . . . with his knees!

Suddenly, his legs bowed, letting go of the wheel. He squirted semen into her mouth. Laura was taken aback by how unsavory it tasted. Byron's potion had been sweet like orange blossoms. The concoction presently in her mouth seemed tinged with cigar smoke.

The Slovenian Beast was groaning and lost control of the car. The Outlander skidded across the right lane and headed toward a ditch alongside the road. Damjan jammed the brakes just in time. Laura whipped away from him and coughed up his semen onto the seat. He pumped the final drops of milky fluid from his manhood. It was to Laura a gargantuan radish, uprooted from the earth and raw.

A rectangular object boogied in Damjan's pants pocket. He took out his cell phone, glanced at the display, and exhaled in exacerbation.

"Allo?" He proceeded to speak to the caller in Italian. During the conversation, his tone transitioned from blatant annoyance to forced affection. He clicked off.

"Who was that?" Laura asked.

"My wife," he replied.

CHAPTER 26:
PARTY IN PRAGUE

Byron's heart nearly leaped out of his chest when he saw not only the country code for the U.S., but also the city code for Chicago pop up on his mobile phone display. It must be Laura!

"*Geliebte?*" Byron asked expectantly.

"Oh, I'm sorry. I must have the wrong—"

"Laura?"

"No. This isn't Laura. I'm a friend of hers. She gave me your number. Is this Byron Baumgaarten?" Her voice was upbeat and crystal clear through the global network. The American accent and melodic cadences were familiar to him. Unfortunately, the woman calling him was not Laura.

"Yes, this is Byron. Is Laura okay?"

"Oh, yes. Laura is great!" The girl said enthusiastically. "This is Jolene Peters. I'm an American artist living in Prague. Laura suggested that I contact you regarding representation. We're both from Chicago."

At that moment, Byron felt that the Czech Republic, Austria, Slovakia, and Germany—indeed all of the countries of Central and Eastern Europe—were gusted up in a cyclone and spinning him back to her and home.

*

Thirty-six hours hence, he was standing against a brick wall with a bottle of beer numbing his hands. It was after midnight. The party in Prague was underway and he was dead tired. He had flown in from Berlin that morning, hoping to track Laura down. It had been a tortuous ordeal extricating himself from Zsa Zsa. Literally. The night before, she had dug her squared fingernails into his skin.

Jolene had been his decoy. Knowing that Byron was always on the lookout for new talent, Zsa Zsa easily fell into the trap. The young artist threatened to knock Her Majesty off her throne. Immediately, she was jealous of Jolene.

Not as simply, he had to find a way to ward off her amorous advances. When Zsa Zsa begged for sex on his final night in Germany, he countered, "No. It undermines the art dealer code of ethics." How had he come up with that one?

She wasn't buying the newfangled doctrine. "That has never stopped you in the past. Are you already sleeping with the nymph?"

"No, no, of course not. We haven't even met each other . . . yet." He allowed guilt to infiltrate the tone of his voice. It was to deter Zsa Zsa from focusing on the real object of his desire, Laura.

Since seeing the city code for Chicago, 312, Byron had one wish: To be reunited with Laura. A night of sex with the Wicked Witch of Eastern Europe might put a dark spell on his odyssey.

In the end, Byron prevailed by pretending to fall asleep. Zsa Zsa's incessant harping could do that to a person.

He knew that there was an untoward side to his role as rescuer. Who did he think he was? He knew the man he wanted to be: A caped and crusading Schindler (the good German who in WWII had saved thousands of Jews). He envisioned himself scooping up his fragile girlfriend and freeing her from the Nazis.

Where was she, anyway? Jolene had said that she and Laura were friends. Was he wrong to assume that she would be at this party?

"Would you like to see my drawings?" The artist interrupted his thoughts.

"I'd love to."

Jolene led Byron to one of the bedrooms. He surveyed the

setting of the debut. The haphazard furnishings of stacked beds and computers suggested that as many as four graduate students lived in these tight quarters. He was glad that he was not one of them.

On the top bunk bed, Jolene had installed her series, *Café Life*. Each canvas was roughly three feet in height and barely fit in the space between mattress and ceiling. To the tops of the bedposts, she had clamped spotlights.

"My boyfriend, Leo, let me borrow his movie lights. He's a filmmaker. I tested them earlier. He calls them his 'babies.' Who knows why?"

"I think that is their technical name."

"Really?"

Byron nodded and smiled at her innocence.

Jolene faded up the intensity of the lamps. They shone on the glimmering oily sketches.

"Voilà!"

*

Why isn't he saying anything? Jolene began to feel dread. A knot was forming in her stomach. Her work must be too pedestrian for him. She was not avant-garde enough. This audition of sorts was a non-starter. Jolene knew it in that 99 percent reliable gut of hers.

"Here you are!" Leo sidled up beside Joey. His muscles bulged. His choice of clothing was, quite frankly, embarrassing. He had on a t-shirt with big block lettering that read, "DIE HIPSTER SCUM." Normally, she agreed with the credo, but tonight . . .

"So, are you going to sign my girlfriend?"

Must he be so blunt? This whole experience was turning into an exercise in humiliation.

*

Byron was speechless.

It was the night of the Summer Equinox, the longest day of the year. Something ineffable was happening at this party in Prague. He had come here, expecting to see Laura. Instead, he was encountering a different otherworldly beauty.

Typically, the art he evaluated for sale fell into two categories. It was brazen and conceptual, bereft of human emotions, or untrained attempts at representation. Due to buyer demand, he generally signed the former. In either case, there was no evidence that the artist could actually draw from life models.

The series consisted of panels that when placed side by side formed a panorama of a Prague hotspot. For inspiration, Jolene had selected the Globe Café, the exact place where Byron had met Laura.

Triptychs, three related paintings, were common during the Renaissance, primarily in Christian art. Jolene went beyond the tradition by utilizing five connected mattes and depicting contemporary subjects. The two on the left were of Prague fashion models and young entrepreneurs. The two on the right were of Bohemian artists and working class locals. All four were archetypes immortalized in the Globe Café. She brought the figures to life with a vivid pallet and expressive brushstrokes.

For Byron, it was the center panel of two lovers that took his breath away. They could have been—and possibly were—Laura and Byron in the Globe Café on that first fateful day.

All he could say was, "Where is Laura?"

*

"I'm sorry. She's not here." Had Jolene made a tactical error in pushing her off to Ljubljana with Damjan? If not for Laura, this meeting never would have happened.

"I must thank her. Your art is exquisite."

Jolene ventured, "Does that mean—?"

"If you are asking me, am I a fan? The answer is a resounding yes."

Could he be any nicer? Jolene felt a smile break out on her face. The art dealer was also beaming. "Thank you!" she cried.

"I would love to be your agent if, of course, *you* will have *me*."

"Yes! *I* would love to be *your* client."

"I already have in mind a gallery that will want to show your drawings. It is in Paris."

"Paris!" Jolene saw her life changing before her eyes.

"Are you free on Monday? Say two p.m.? We can meet then to review the terms of the contract."

"Yes. Monday is great. Four p.m. would better. I can leave my job an hour early. I work in the Municipal House."

"Four p.m. it is then. I know the location. There is a café on the first level. How about we meet there?"

"Fabulous. You've got it."

"See you then," said Leo.

Joey turned to him. "I thought you were shooting your movie on Monday," she said.

"I'll be done by four, no problem."

Was he *jealous*? She turned to Byron. "How do you know Laura?"

A faraway emotional look crossed his face, and Jolene immediately knew the answer. He was in love with her. In affairs of the heart, her intuition was 100 percent correct.

She recalled the items on Laura's list: Find a Job (Done! Thanks to Jo!), Call Dad (Had she?), and Find a New Boyfriend. Was Byron the old boyfriend and Damjan the new? Jolene cringed at the possibility. She had saved the napkin that contained Laura's list and Byron's number. *The three of us are forever linked*, thought Jolene.

"We met in Prague and have done some traveling together," Byron said. "I thought she might be here tonight."

"She went out of town for the weekend."

"Where did she go?"

"Ljubljana."

"Ljubljana? Why? Why on earth would she go to Ljubljana? Is she alone?"

"She went for work. We work together."

"You do? I did not know Laura had a job."

"The operation is a tad shady if you ask me," interjected Leo.

No one is asking you, especially when I am the one paying the bills, thought Jolene. "Yes, we both work in advertising."

"She did that in the States."

"You should see her in action. She's amazing."

"I know." Byron sighed.

Jolene thought of her friend, with her wavy, long blonde hair and ever-present smile. She pictured her standing right here, next to Byron, her new and kind ally.

Laura and Byron: They were meant to be together.

Laura and Damjan: That was all wrong.

"She'll be back soon. You can see her when we meet on Monday." She took Leo's hand and squeezed it tight.

CHAPTER 27:
LJUBLJANA

"You can park here?" asked a dubious Laura.

"I know the owner."

It was near midnight when Damjan drove up to the sparkling office plaza in the center of Ljubljana and illegally parked his SUV on the concrete portico. He proudly pointed to the skyscraper that rose from the commercial development and towered over the city. "It's the tallest building in Ljubljana."

They headed on foot down a steep road. Three rowdy men walked alongside them. One of the grubby guys opened up his trousers to pee. The other two brandished about their cloaked penises, jokingly imitating their friend.

"They're disgusting!"

"On this point, I quite agree with you." Damjan put his arm around her and dragged her away. He covered one of her eyes to shield her partially from the drunks.

"They are no doubt from Italy, my wife's country. How embarrassing for me that this is your first impression of my native land. You will see for yourself that Ljubljana can withstand the debasements of its foreign visitors."

When they reached the bottom of the hill, Damjan took her hand. They stood before a trio of stony bridges traversing a stagnant river. Something in the air made Laura think that this is what Prom Night must be like in Slovenia.

"Throw away your travel books, Laura. You now have me, Damjan, for your tour guide. Here, we have the Triple Bridge. On the other side of the river is the Old Village."

An Old Village rendered very new, Laura observed. While the

buildings dated from the Middle Ages, they housed some of the same brand name boutiques found in neighborhoods from the West Loop of Chicago to South Beach in Miami, from Paris to Prague, from London to . . . well, Ljubljana.

Music thumped from underground. There was a nightclub in the embankment. Young partiers were queuing up. Damjan bypassed the velvet rope, paid off the bouncer, and escorted Laura inside.

The dance floor was empty, while the crowd clamored outside. "Stay here while I get us drinks. Don't go away."

She waited in the middle of the round disco. Videos of the Big Three—Britney, Christina, and an ageless Madge—were projected onto screens. The DJ was playing "Into the Groove" by Madonna. Laura leaned into the curvilinear wall.

It occurred to her that at this very moment, Byron might also be resting against a wall at the party in Prague.

She was in the *wrong* place at the *right* time. Or was she? A mini movie of Byron materialized in her mind. He was alone. He was holding a beer bottle, with condensation forming on the brown glass, in a roomful of young expats and Prague locals. As her mental lens zoomed out, the viewfinder took in Zsa Zsa. Her voluminous black hair brushed against her bosom. She was digging her fingernails into his arm. Now, she was reaching for his balls. No! Stop! Cut to black!

Better to be in this room, even with Damjan in the next. She tried to relax by letting the ephemeral images of the three pop stars shimmer on her white dress. They were a rainbow of particles. She felt the drumbeat in her stomach. The melody lifted her spirit. At her core, Laura was an American girl.

The music and videos were so overexposed in the States that they were shunned in both fringy and mainstream clubs. Here in Ljubljana, the same unhip entertainment rendered the place the center of the universe.

Damjan reappeared, carrying two glasses filled to their brims with lime green liquid and white foam. A flamingo stirrer stood in each drink. "Here you are, my woman."

His woman? Where did he get off assuming this? *Of course,* thought Laura. It was due to the blow-his-mind blow job. Laura would go along with this charade until she could turn Damjan into the police. Until then, she needed him to trust her completely.

Laura took one of the drinks from him. With the first few sips, her impetuous feelings for Damjan flooded over her. The disco lights were flashing on his body. Damjan's bronzed chest burst out of a roughly hewn shirt. He daintily held the tropical girlie drink.

He winked at Laura. It was a flirtatious gesture that was so *not him.* She felt the unknown substances in the glowing concoction going to her head and to her dismay, elsewhere.

Damjan screamed, "Insipid idiots!"

"Is that plural or singular?" She was not sure if he was talking about the horde of people that had just entered or her.

"What?" he shouted.

"Who are you talking about?"

"Them! Their biggest tragedy is that we lost our beaches to Croatia. This is all you ever hear from them. That we should not have given up our shoreline when Slovenia was carved out from Yugoslavia. They will be complaining about this until they go to their graves."

At the morbid reference, the music switched to a disco dirge. It was "Our Love" by Donna Summer. The song induced in Laura an overwhelming sadness. Her longing for Byron was suddenly so palpable she could feel it in every inch of her body.

Laura was inclined to slither down to the floor and burst into tears. What good would that do her? As a counteroffensive, she shouted at Damjan: "Do you want to dance?"

"As you might imagine, I am a clumsy dancer."

"I am no Ginger Rogers."

"Do you dare me to make a fool of myself?"

"I dare you!"

He swigged the final drops. Laura had stopped drinking after the first rush of alcohol. They set their glasses on the floor, not caring that within seconds the delicate stemware would be trampled.

Damjan danced by moving only his upper body. His shoulders and chest shimmied to the beat. He stared at Laura as she bopped. Her routine was a mishmash of sixties go-go girl and punk pogo sticking. It reflected her age bracket, the tail end of the Baby Boom and not quite Generation X. She was expending far more energy than he. Damjan was more focused on Laura than his own dancing. She assumed that he was imagining her dancing in the nude.

Beyond Damjan, Laura caught sight of a uniformed official. He was dressed in full military regalia. Either he was a member of the Slovenian army or this was how the local Ljubljana police went about. He was animatedly talking to one of the bouncers.

Laura believed that this was her chance for escape. She must sneak away and try to speak with him. Hopefully, he knew English.

It could boomerang, worried Laura. Damjan was friends with the guy responsible for the only skyscraper in downtown Ljubljana and presumably the owner of this club. Why not law enforcement? He had breezed past the thugs guarding the disco. He could park wherever he damn well pleased. Why not be allowed to freely traipse around Ljubljana with 100,000 Euros in stolen cash?

Laura could be arrested for assisting him in the theft. She knew nothing of the Slovenian judicial system. There was no guarantee that she would be offered immunity in exchange for coming forward with the truth.

Nothing is guaranteed, thought Laura. She recalled the crash and burn ending of her Chicago advertising career, her devastating breakup with Byron, and the death of her beloved mother. The death of her mother had taught her one lesson: That love transcends one's physical time on this planet. "She will always be with you, guiding you and telling you what to do," her older female coworkers had consoled her in her days of grief. Over the years, Laura had come to see the meaning of their words.

"I need to use the restroom," she now said.

Damjan frowned.

She headed for the lobby, in the direction of the officer whose overcoat was bedecked with badges. He must be a hero of the Balkan Wars.

Eureka! Go to the American Embassy! A jewel of an idea had manifested itself. Laura stopped in her tracks and pivoted.

Yes! She would lock herself in a cubicle in the ladies' room. She would call someone, anyone, for the number of the American Embassy in Slovenia. All of her essential items—her phone, passport, credit cards, and money (along with her eyeliner, mascara, and lip gloss)—were in her purse. It was a hard metal, heart shaped silver case that hung from a matching chain across her body. The purse had belonged to her mother. Laura felt that the revelation of what to do had also come from her mother.

It was too late.

Two fists tightened around her arms and yanked her back against a firm chest. His particular male scent and blistering body heat were all too familiar to her.

"Laura love lily. Where are you going?" He tugged on the tufts of her hair.

He dragged her outdoors to the banks of the Ljubljana River. He lifted her from the ground. "I should throw you into the river."

"Put me down."

"As you request," he replied. "There is no point to tossing you in. The waters are shallow and you will not drown."

"I would not drown anyway. I know how to swim."

"I am sure you do. Lessons at the country club, I presume. Your parents would have done well by flinging you overboard from their yacht. It would have been sink or sin."

"Don't you mean sink or swim?"

"Yes, yes!" He broke into laughter at his gaffe. "On second

thought, look at how you turned out. You are a sinful girl."

"We have something in common, Damjan."

He laughed again. Maybe he was not that angry after all.

They retraced their steps up the hill and to the skyscraper. Potted plants were all that stood on the plaza. The Outlander was gone.

"What the hell?" He pirouetted in the vacant space, clutching his head. "You did this, Laura!"

"I did no such thing."

"I should have known better than to leave you alone in the disco. You took the opportunity to betray me when I was getting us our drinks."

She *should* have used the time so wisely. "No, Damjan. It wasn't me. It wasn't anyone. You parked illegally. Your car was probably towed."

"Impossible!"

"I am sure the police have your car."

"My car and everything else!"

"We should go get it."

"*We* should go get it? No. We are no longer a team of equals. The stakes are too great. From now on, you will do as I say."

Whatever you say, thought Laura. She had been obeying his every command up until a few minutes ago. It was what had gotten them into trouble in the first place.

Red and white cabs were parked along the curb, with no place to go at two a.m. Except for the first cab in the lineup, whose driver was dozing, they were empty. Laura thought she could make a break for it. She imagined dashing into the backseat, shouting at the driver, "Go now!" and the night air whipping her in the face as she escaped to freedom.

Damjan seized her upper arm. "I know what you're thinking. Don't. I said we are no longer a team of *equals*. We are a *team* nonetheless." He pushed one finger into the small of her back, in simulation of a gun. With his other hand, he pinched both sides of her neck. He was hurting and scaring her. He directed her away from the business district and to a less developed part of Ljubljana.

"You must forgive me, Laura love lily." He was still poking and pushing her. "You go your own way. I am not used to an independent woman."

Laura had been yielding to a fault. How much more compliance did he expect from her? "What about your wife?"

"She is not my wife. She's my ex."

"Since when?"

"Two years we have been estranged. I will not subject you to the nasty language needed to describe her. With you, it is different. You have an excuse. You are an American. It is understandable. It is ingrained in your renegade culture."

"We also have, 'Stand by Your Man'," she said.

"Stand by your man? What is that?"

"An old country 'n' western song."

"My mother stood by my father to the death."

"They stood up to a totalitarian regime. It was for a higher principle."

"Do not discredit what we do. We are destined for a higher place. One with lots of money that you helped me earn." He laughed.

They had been trudging through a foggy drizzle. In the near distance, barracks painted in a hodgepodge of colors shone.

"Here we are." He let go of her neck and dropped his pointed finger from her back. They walked side by side the rest of the way.

Weary backpackers were checking in. Damjan told her that a talented Slovenian architect (another friend, he claimed) had remade the war prison into a youth hostel.

There was one room left. They took it. It was smaller than her closet at home. Home, as in Chicago, thought Laura. The furnishings were austere, consisting mainly of a white futon bed on a bleached birch floor. The designer had left the metal bars on the one window. In metaphoric juxtaposition, he had installed a skylight in the ceiling. It inspired thoughts of flight. Rain drummed on the glass pane.

Damjan took away her purse, confiscating from Laura her phone, passport, credit cards, and money. He scattered her makeup on the bed. He exited through a set of two doors. The first one was the original gate from the jail cell. He turned the key and locked her in. "I can no longer trust you," he said. "Such is the inevitable dynamic between the sexes. Now I will get my car."

CHAPTER 28:

MANIC MONDAY

On Monday morning, when Jolene showed up for work, the employees that had arrived before her were already turning around and going home.

"We can't get in."

"The place is deserted."

"We called Damjan on his cell and he won't answer."

"He owes us money!"

"This can't be." Jolene brushed past her coworkers. She peered through the glass at the darkened office. The chrome cubicles were barely discernible. Uselessly, she banged on the door. Where was Damjan? Where was Laura?

She went downstairs. It was pouring outside. They were predicting the most rainfall since the Prague floods of 2002. From the lobby, she watched the rivulets of water inundate the streets and sidewalks.

Her call to Laura went straight to voice mail. "Hey, Laura! It's me, Jolene. Call me as soon as you get this message. It's important. I need to know that you are okay." Frustrated, she clicked off and tried Leo.

"Hey, Joey. What's up?"

"I'm at work. Only no one else is here. The place is abandoned. Everything is locked up."

"What did I tell you? I've been saying all along that the guy is a slime ball."

"I know. I know. You were right."

"You should have listened to me."

"I know. I said you were right."

"He probably ran off with all of the money you made for him."

"Worse. My friend, Laura, is with him. On Friday, he invited her to go to Ljubljana. I encouraged her to go. I just tried calling her. She's not answering her phone."

"It's not your problem, Joey. From what you told me, she was in on his scam. Didn't you say that she was really good?"

"No. Laura didn't know. She may be in trouble."

"She likes the guy, right?"

"Yes, but—"

"I wouldn't worry about her."

"Laura referred me to Byron. I think I should call him. He will want to know."

"No. Wait. I'm coming to get you."

He hung up before she could say another word.

*

Byron and Jolene were already seated and engrossed in conversation when Leo arrived at the café. Joey stood up and kissed his cheek. Then she announced, "Byron is going to Ljubljana to look for Laura."

"There are no direct flights after seven in the morning," Byron said. "Everything else connects through Rome or Frankfurt. It is a big roundabout. If I leave now, I will not get there until night."

"Take my motorcycle," offered Leo.

"Are you sure?"

"Take it, dude. How far is Ljubljana?"

"Six hundred kilometers, I think."

"You'll be there in no time." Leo pulled the poncho over his head and handed it to Byron. "You're going to need this."

"Thanks."

Byron pushed his arms through the holes of the gauche yellow tarp. It resembled a cape.

"Dude, you look like a super hero!" Leo said.

"I hope Laura thinks so."

"Take this." Leo handed Byron the helmet.

Byron fastened the strap beneath his chin. "How are you two going to get home? You'll get all wet."

"We'll be fine," said Leo.

"We'll share my umbrella," said Jolene.

"I will find a way to repay you. I promise," said Byron.

"You already have." Leo and Joey said it in unison. Leo gave Byron the keys.

"Thanks again." Byron took off.

Once outside, Byron remembered that he had never before operated a motorcycle. Was a special license required? The roads were treacherous. He had no map. He turned the key. The engine roared and music boomed. He located the gear shifter and, most importantly, the brakes! Cautiously, he backed out of the space. He applied the turn signal and started down the street. He was on his way!

He would follow the signs for Austria and points south. As he merged onto the highway, gravel flew up from the cars and hit his elbows and his knees. Passing trucks caused subsonic reverberations in his chest.

He was not reliving his youth. His rebellious bad boy nature was relatively new. Throughout most of his adult life, he had led the life of a scholarly art critic. Zsa Zsa had cracked his conservative shell. For this and nothing more, he was indebted to her. His heart belonged to Laura.

The storm diminished to a drizzle and the traffic thinned. He could finally make out the melody and lyrics of the music. Brahms it was not.

The song was familiar, possibly by a British band from the eighties. This had never been his kind of music. He preferred chamber ensembles to synthesized pop.

And yet . . .

A sudden key change rendered the piece intense and pining. *Let this be my soundtrack*, thought Byron, as the rolling green landscape opened up to him and he continued along the now-barren road, leading to the Balkans.

CHAPTER 29:
HOSTEL ENVIRONMENT

Her condo in Chicago was on the fourth floor. Outside, next to her open bedroom window, birds chirped. Without looking, Laura knew that a bevy of them had settled on the treetops. A cool breeze flowed through the screen. It was not yet dawn. Her eyes flickered open. A tulle canopy was overhead. She glanced over at Byron, who was sleeping and at her side. It was perfect.

A hot and heavy mass steamrolled her. Her vision was shrouded in the darkness. Her heart was beating as her consciousness shifted states. Laura realized that she had been dreaming. Damjan was on top of her. He must have returned while she was sleeping. He was passionately kissing her neck. Laura interpreted this to mean that his mission had been a success: That he had reclaimed his vehicle and the 95,000 Euros without incident.

Laura could feel his uncut meat growing hard. She was trapped beneath his heaviness. He relieved her by placing some of the weight on one of his elbows. From this position, he was able to maneuver his hotdog between her thighs, which were sticky from the humidity. Damjan pushed it up her hole and moaned. His white crew neck t-shirt seemed to be strangling him. Impulsively, Laura pulled it over his head, signaling to him that she was a willing participant. In truth, she did not know what she was.

His groans were loud enough to wake up everyone in the youth hostel. She bunched up the shirt and shoved it in his mouth. He chewed on it, twisting his head and grunting like an animal. As he went at her, it occurred to Laura that on a base instinctual level, she knew Damjan better than she knew Byron. That did not mean that she liked what she knew. In response to his manly friction, her body unwillingly surrendered, first in surprising ripples and then in an uncontrollable tidal wave. Her screams brought on his triumphant finale.

Whatever this was, it was purely primordial. Of one thing Laura was certain: It was not love.

His sweaty bulk stayed on her for a few moments. He brushed her hair off her forehead. Then he moved his body some inches—but not completely—off her.

"Goodnight." He started to snore.

How was she going to get out of here? The slightest move might disturb him.

She stared up at the skylight. Rain continued to fall on the sloping window. Globs of water landed, stabilized, and eventually pushed off like a downhill skiers.

What had Damjan done with her purse? She attempted to wriggle out from under him, incrementally shifting his hairy arm, which rested languorously over her chest. This took Laura a good five minutes, as she was cautious not to rouse him. Once out of bed, she noiselessly surveyed the room. Gingerly, she lifted his trousers off the floor to reveal her purse! Its jeweled surface—glittering in a sliver of moonlight—once again called to mind her mother, the fashionista.

The purse had a sturdy metal clasp. Carelessly opening and closing it would disrupt the silence. Little by little, she released the catch, cupping her hand to mute any sound.

In the opened pouch, she saw that her phone, passport, credit cards, and money were intact, just as she had left them. She quietly closed the purse and slung it over her shoulder. She explored his pants, feeling for the jagged keys buried in one of the pockets. She fished them out, being careful not to jangle them.

She tried inserting each key into the keyhole to unlock the prison door. The fourth and final one was the charm. It easily slid into the serrated hole. Voilà! She turned the key ninety degrees.

Clang! The sharp noise resounded in the hostel hallway.

Damjan grunted and mumbled something garbled and incomprehensible. She opened the creaky gate and ran out of the room with purse in hand.

"Laura!"

His voice bellowed down the hallway. The thumping of his footsteps followed.

He caught up with her, in an area once guarded by the Germans and later, the Soviet Military Police. Unlike his forbearers, Damjan lacked the dignity of a uniform or, for that matter, any clothes whatsoever. His fiend flapped during the short sprint and settled into the morass between his legs when he came to a standstill.

"Where are you going?" he asked her.

"I need to use the ladies' room."

"Why are you carrying that?" He indicated her purse.

"This?"

"Yes."

"It's that time of the month," she improvised.

"You mean you are unclean? Why didn't you say something?"

"It happened so fast."

"I would like to take a look."

"Are you serious?"

He burst out laughing. "No. Not there. I wouldn't dare. This," he said, wrenching the purse. He peered into it. He removed her cell phone.

"Where are, you know, the—"

"—products?"

"Yes."

"I don't have them. It just started. I was unprepared. Maybe you did this to me, Damjan," she suggested with a phony smile.

"I suppose it is possible. Why bring the purse if there are no, as you say, products?"

"I was going to buy them in there, in the ladies' room. There should be machines."

"You expect to buy them with this?" He held up her credit card.
"Sure."

"Where do you think you are? This is not the United States of
Credit Happy Consumers. This is Slovenia."

"Fine. I need the proper currency."

"I will oblige you." He turned back to the room, with her purse
and all its vital contents.

He came back with his pants on, the belt buckle undone. He offered
her a handful of foreign coins. "Here. Go. Knock yourself out."

*

For the next twenty-four hours, Damjan held Laura in close
captivity. He brought in food and walked her to and from the
bathroom. She complained that he was treating her like a dog.

On the second day (she determined it was Sunday), she begged
him to let her bathe. He did not trust her to be out of his sight
for more than a minute. He put orange cones in front of the
unoccupied male restroom so that no one else could enter. She
undressed and got in the shower stall designated for men. Damjan
stood fully dressed, leaning against the wall, with his arms folded
across his chest. He surveyed every inch of her as she lathered and
rinsed her body and hair.

Believing that she had her period, he did not touch her. For a
few days, she enjoyed a reprieve from his physical attentions. His
peering eyes, however, created unwanted tingling sensations on
her wet skin.

On the third day (Manic Monday, thought Laura), she
suggested that they take a walk. She was deliberately nonchalant in
her proposal. She accurately calculated that he was growing as stir
crazy as she was. With much magnanimity, he agreed to the walk
and more. He would show her Ljubljana's top tourist attractions, its

London style-park and the National Art Gallery of Slovenia.

Once outdoors, Laura breathed in the fresh smell of wet grass. The long rains had finally stopped. Yet gray clouds continued to dominate the sky. Similarly, in the museum, the paintings were dark and brooding. Despite being in the South of Europe, Slovenia was neither sunny nor carefree. The art commentary—clumsily translated into English—was weighty and serpentine, demanding her uninterrupted concentration.

As she tried diligently to comprehend the text, Damjan studied her. She asked him, "Do you understand any of this? Maybe it is clearer in Slovene."

"You need a Ph.D. in epistemology. The Slovenian intelligentsia has—as you say in English—their heads up their asses."

"So, I am not stupid?"

He laughed. "No."

Afterwards, he brought her to a working class restaurant in Ljubljana's Old Village. He ordered for the both of them, plates of beef and a bottle of red wine. It was the most delicious meat she had ever eaten. *Let them eat steak*, thought Laura. Was it due to superior Slovenian cooking or her ravenous hunger? She was famished for normalcy and freedom. This meal, this day, had given her hope that Damjan was relenting.

"Tomorrow, we upgrade our accommodations," he announced.

"Here, here," she said, raising her wineglass.

"Ljubljana has a new hotel. It is top of the line in every regard. We will have our privacy and all luxuries, including a fifty-two inch TV screen. Does this please you, Laura love lily?"

"Yes. Thank you, Damjan." His glass was empty and she took the liberty of refilling it.

"By that time, you should be ready for me, no?" He smiled slyly.

She knew what he meant by that. "I may be ready for you. When are we going back to Prague?"

"Never." Seeing her defeated expression, he added, "We never go back to Prague. Once we complete our business here, we travel to Venice and Milan."

"What about your wife? Isn't she in Italy?"

"Why is she a concern to you? I told you. We are estranged."

"She calls you." Just then, Laura heard a joyful and familiar melody. She had downloaded the ringtone version of "Vacation" by the Go-Go's. No Eastern European person would be so inclined to have the same ringtone.

"Someone is calling me. Let me see who it is." The tune faded out.

He held it up to her so she could read the number of the missed call.

Laura's heart skipped a beat. *Oh no*, she thought.

"Who is looking for you?" He placed the phone in his front shirt pocket.

"My dad," she replied. "Give me the phone. I need to call him back."

He just smirked.

"Damjan, give me the phone."

Inside his sheer white shirt pocket, the cell phone blinked neon colors. It beeped, signifying a message.

"Please, Damjan. I should have called him a long time ago."

"This is not my problem."

She reached across the table for her phone. He swatted her arm. In so doing, he knocked over the empty wine bottle. It shattered on the floor.

The waiter immediately brought over and uncorked a new bottle, replacing the broken, already depleted one. Damjan ceremoniously sniffed the cork. He swilled and tasted the wine. Shards of glass were still at their feet.

Holding back her tears, Laura watched Damjan drink one brimming goblet after another, until he polished off the second bottle. She was disillusioned that he did not pass out at the table.

He staggered back to their hostel. This was no easy feat as his rugged shoes kept getting stuck in the mushy ground. Back in their room, Damjan squinted to make out the small buttons on his shirt. He swaggered as he undressed, performing an unintentional striptease. He draped the shirt on the desk chair and left on his trousers. He locked the door and placed the keys back in his pants pocket. Clothed from the waist down, he stretched out on the futon.

"Come to bed, Laura love lily." He patted a place beside him, for her. She stayed sitting on the edge of the mattress. Before long, the sound of his boisterous snoring filled the room. She jumped up, went right for Damjan's shirt pocket, and retrieved her cell phone. She illuminated the display.

Her father had called twice. Jolene had called five times.

There was also a text message. It read: "*Geliebte* where R U?"

CHAPTER 30:
JOY TO THE WORLD

"*Geliebte?*" Laura realized that she had said the German word for lover out loud. She glanced up at Damjan to be sure that he did not stir.

The text had to be from Byron. Where was *she?* Where was *he?* She excitedly typed the excruciatingly long name, L J U B L J A N A, and hit send. Her phone hissed like a rattlesnake. She quickly covered it with her hands to muffle the sound.

She glanced at Damjan. Fortunately, the Slovenian Beast was a sound sleeper, when drunk. She set her phone to mute. Laura waited and waited for Byron to reply. It felt like an eternity. Maybe he was out of cell phone range. She stared at her phone in the palm of her hand, willing it to vibrate.

Damjan's snoring suddenly stopped. For several seconds, there was no breathing. Was he dead? He expelled a large guffaw. He was loud enough to awaken himself. His eyes blinked open and he looked at her from across the room. "Huh?" he asked.

"I didn't say anything."

"What are you doing?"

At this point, her phone buzzed. She had forgotten about this feature associated with the vibration mode.

To obscure the noise, she shouted at him. "I'm coming to bed really soon. I'm getting undressed right now."

"What's taking you so long?"

"Nothing. You fell asleep immediately. As soon as you hit the sack."

"I see. Hurry it up."

Laura turned her back to Damjan and began pulling her dress over her head. Surreptitiously, she illuminated the phone display while underneath the garment.

The text read, "I am here 2 4 U. Coming to get U. Where in L?"

In disbelief, Laura looked at the small screen. He is here, too? In Ljubljana? He had come to get her?

Laura yearned to respond to him, but how? She lowered the dress back over her body and stared at Damjan. He was again snoring and appeared to be asleep. She quietly sat down on a stool.

What was the exact name of this place? It was carved into the birch wood vanity. Hostel Cecilia? No. It said Cellica, as in Jail Cell.

"Hostel Cellica," she typed and hit send. His reply was almost instantaneous.

"I'm there."

Laura was joyous.

How long would it take him to get here? Laura settled in for a ten to fifteen minute wait.

She envisioned Byron cruising through downtown Ljubljana in the back of a cab. This could be her opportunity not only for escape, but to have Damjan apprehended for grand larceny (or the Slovenian legal equivalent). She continued to text Byron: "Room 115." Send! She pecked away: "Bring P O L I Z E I." Send!

*

Unbeknownst to Laura, Byron had been in Ljubljana since the late afternoon. He had texted her as soon as he had arrived. When she did not reply, he assumed that she was ignoring him. Could he blame her, given the Zsa Zsa fiasco? He had behaved deplorably. He imagined that Laura and this Damjan fellow were sexing it up the entire time he was riding up and down the bumpy cobble streets of Ljubljana, in search of her. His bottom was sore, but he could not bring himself to get off Leo's motorcycle.

Once you've seen one Old Village you've seen them all, thought Byron. He had eyes for only Laura, for her long, straggly blonde hair and thin, curving body. For that initial image that had so enthralled him in the Globe Café.

She was nowhere to be found.

He decided to try the outer edge of town, reaching an infirmary that bore an illuminated green cross. What if something unthinkable had happened to her?

He parked the motorcycle, but did not get off. He pulled out the phone from the front pocket of his jacket. There it was at last, her one word reply and acknowledgement. "Ljubljana." He texted back. She answered, "Hostel Cellica." He knew where that was. Across the street. He revved up the bike and sped off.

*

Laura heard the roar of an engine. She went to the box window, climbed on the recessed ledge, and looked out. There he was! That was quick! Where had he gotten the motorcycle? He took off the helmet. He ran across the unpaved parking lot, while glancing up at the windows without seeing her.

Byron! He was coming to her rescue! He looked so dashing! Should she put on some makeup? Surely, she had gone to seed over the past few days. It seemed to be part of her punishment, to be reduced to unattractiveness. Damjan guarding her each morning in the lavatory had severely limited her beauty regimen.

My looks should be my greatest worry, thought Laura. Where was the P O L I Z E I?

*

At the Hostel Cellica lobby, Byron described Laura to a gangly clerk. He had a swath of black bangs across his forehead and blunt studs through his mouth and ears.

"I think I know her. She checked in a few nights ago with a thug of a man. Ljubljana Mafia, if you ask me."

Byron flinched. "She's in danger. He may be holding her in captivity."

The clerk became wide eyed. "Would you like to go have a look-see?"

"Yes. Yes. Please."

The clerk looked up the room number and grabbed the proper keys. They climbed a flight of stairs. As their footsteps echoed in the seemingly endless hall, Byron's anxiety increased. It was possible that Laura was not being held against her will. Deep down, she might actually desire this "thug of a man." Or that after all they had been through, she was through with him. Could he blame her?

*

Laura looked askance, down the hallway and in the direction of the footsteps. She stood grasping the metal bars of the inner door to her room. Hopefully, Damjan would not reawaken in time to question her. Her pink backpack was squarely on her back. She had furiously and noiselessly packed up her belongings. At long last, Byron and the desk clerk came into full view.

When their eyes met, for one singular beautiful moment, her surroundings—the war prison turned boutique hostel, the young, pierced employee, the hulk sleeping in the bed behind them— along with one painful memory, of Zsa Zsa and the bizarre threesome in Berlin, fell away. It was just the two of them. It was the way Laura hoped it would be, always.

"Laura. How are you?"

"Great. Now that you're here." He touched her fingers through the gate.

The desk clerk unlocked the door. Laura stepped out of the cell. When she did, she felt a dip in the floor beneath her feet. She was free.

*

"Laura!" Laura glanced over her shoulder and saw Damjan charging after them. He was shirtless.

"Quick!" They dashed into the stairwell and hurried down the steps, the thick metal door slamming behind them. Laura asked, "Did you call the police?"

"No."

"Why not?"

"I—" Byron began.

"Did you get my text message?"

"No."

Did you sleep with Zsa Zsa? She was tempted to inquire, hoping to go zero for three. Instead, Laura abandoned her questioning (and jealousy) at the bottom of the steps. They heaved through weighty double doors and emerged in the lobby. "We need to call the police. *Now!*"

Damjan burst through the metal doors. Laura was still holding her cell phone and was about to dial 911. Was 911 the emergency number in Slovenia? She gazed up at the hostel employee, who was hopefully a Ljubljana local and not a newbie. He ought to know how to contact the cops.

Damjan wrenched her arm. As he was yanking her outside, she shouted at the clerk, "Call!"

Byron ran after them. "Let her go!"

Damjan snatched her hair and twisted her head. She smelled alcohol on his breath. Byron leaped at Damjan's back and tried to pull him away from her.

Damjan turned around and threw a punch at him. Byron ducked. The hurling fist widely missed him. Damjan staggered. Laura realized that he was still woozy from the second bottle of wine he had had at dinner about an hour ago.

He came back at her, this time looping his arm around her neck. He bent his elbow to squeeze her throat. Byron tried to loosen the grip. With his free hand and at close proximity, Damjan socked the shorter man in the face.

Laura screamed. Byron stumbled back. She struggled to be free of Damjan. He dragged her to the Outlander. Laura became aware of an alien wailing sound. It went from soft to strident. Damjan stopped and looked for the source of the siren. As he did, Byron hauled a blow at his naked stomach. Damjan howled and crouched. Byron threw another punch at his head. Damjan slumped against the side of the Outlander.

Two Ljubljana police cars skidded into the parking lot. They screeched to a stop. With their front bumpers touching, the vehicles formed a forty-five degree angle. Two cops got out and grabbed and shoved handcuffs on Byron.

"Not him! You've got the wrong guy!"

Damjan was recovering. He straightened up and fumbled for his keys. He opened the front door to the Outlander and started the ignition.

"You must stop him!" She cried desperately, realizing that the Ljubljana police did not understand English.

Laura ran and grasped the door handle. She managed to pull open the door as Damjan began to take off. She tried to yank him from the car. Her fingertips pinched his arm. It was once again her flesh against his flesh. As they touched, he stopped, turned his head, and resolutely gazed down at her.

"Cunt," he said and hit the gas.

Laura fell on the jagged stones of the parking lot. She heard someone shouting in Slovene and gunshots. The tires blew out. Damjan continued to drive. The vehicle bobbled on all four deflated tires. The policemen ran after him with pistols in hand. Both had abandoned Byron.

With its wheel rims grating on the gravel, the Outlander barely advanced. Damjan jumped out to flee and the officers tackled him to the ground.

The hostel employee was now outside. "Thank you for calling

the police," said Laura.

"Thank you for screaming at them in Slovene," added Byron.

Laura recalled the last time two males had fought over her. She had been twelve years old at the time. The boys played for opposing football teams in her suburban neighborhood. The brouhaha was over for which side Laura—the adolescent sexpot in her butt-length box-pleated skirt—would cheer. The next day, her two suitors strutted through the school, showing off their black eyes and bandaged noses. Laura—the girl over whom they had battled—was no longer on their minds.

How far I've come, mused Laura. She doubted Byron and Damjan would forget this day—or her—anytime soon.

*

Later, at Ljubljana Police Headquarters, there had been a lot of explaining to do. First, Laura, Byron, and the Slovenian hostel worker had to corroborate that Damjan had been the aggressor and provoked the attack, that Byron had thrown the first punch in order to protect Laura from Damjan.

Second, after Laura revealed to the police the hard cases of cold cash stored in the back of the Outlander, Damjan alleged that she had been his willing accomplice. She countered that she had been his *unwitting* accomplice. Her only compensation had been her sales commission. She voluntarily forked over the 5,000 Euros to the cops. Further cooperating with the law, she offered to help return all of the stolen money to the advertisers.

The client information was in Prague. For all she knew, Damjan had deleted the data from his computers and shredded the bank transfers. The Western Union office that they had used in Prague should have the records. Laura suggested this to the police.

The Ljubljana chief of police, who spoke fluent English, countered that such documentation was protected by international privacy laws. Obtaining it would require bureaucratic maneuvering and haggling. It might be months before Western Union was able to release the information.

"I cannot believe I sold advertising for a bogus concert in Budapest," Laura said in exasperation.

"On Saint Margaret's Island?" queried the chief, who was about her age.

"Yes, I think so."

"That is not bogus. It is the biggest summer music festival in all of Europe. My sons will be going."

"Can you help me locate the promoter?" asked Laura. "He might be interested in fulfilling orders for 100,000 Euros worth of ads."

"I'd say so. That's my Laura." Byron took her hand.

They tracked down the concert promoter by phone. He was elated. It turned out that the prices Laura had quoted for the signs closely aligned with his advertising rate card. Hopefully, the client contact info would be intact on Damjan's computers in Prague.

The Ljubljana police chief had listened in on both sides of the phone exchange. He made a duplicate set of the keys to Damjan's office and handed them to Laura. Then, it was just a matter of riding from Ljubljana to Prague on the back of a motorcycle with her arms wrapped around Byron. Not before the chief of police handed her his black police helmet.

"Here you are. You will need this." He was grinning. "Good luck to both of you."

"Thanks!"

CHAPTER 31:
BUDAPEST

Laura's cell phone vibrated against her back, as it was buried somewhere in her backpack. She was riding on the back of a bicycle with her arms wrapped around Byron through the former Jewish Ghetto of Budapest. Even though the crumbling edifices and winding cobblestone roads were nearly one millennium old, the smell of new construction was in the air. The area was covered in dust. The once squalid confines were now being gutted and transformed into upscale lofts and boutiques.

"I'm getting a call," Laura said into Byron's right ear. It was no longer unusual for Laura's cell phone to be ringing in Eastern Europe. It had been five weeks since she first connected the advertisers with the concert promoter and Laura was in hot demand. The promoter had ended up paying her 10 percent commissions and offered her a full time job. It came with a generous expense account and required global traveling. Laura was considering it.

The promoter flew Laura and Byron to Budapest, where she could attend the concert on Saint Margaret's Island and view the sensational, huge electronic signs. As promised, there were hundreds of thousands of young people in the audience. It had been overwhelming for Byron and Laura, the two old fogies. After the first half-day of observing one full, non-repetitive rotation of ad signage, they decided to go sightseeing in Budapest, on a bicycle.

"Why are you slowing down?" she asked.

"Don't you want to see who is calling you?"

In a way, she did not. She did not want a phone call to interrupt the dreamlike state of whipping past romantic Old

World architecture while movie soundtrack music played in her head. "Right. Sure."

Byron pulled the bicycle up to the curb. Laura reluctantly slid off the back, unzipped her backpack, and checked her phone. The missed call was from her dad.

She felt guilty. They had recently chatted, but she had not yet confessed to him any of her escapades or told him about her new boyfriend. She immediately dialed his number.

"Hi, Dad. You just called?"

"I haven't heard from you in a few days. What's going on?" he asked in his usual upbeat voice.

"I'm in Budapest."

"Budapest? What are you doing there? I thought you were in Prague."

"I'm doing some traveling."

"You're not going out at night, are you? I don't like you going out at night alone." This was a long running concern for her father . . . even when she was at home in Chicago.

"No, Dad. I've met someone."

"You have? You mean a man?"

"Yes."

"Who is he?"

"He's an art dealer."

"He's a what?"

"He buys and sells art."

"Oh. I see. Where's he from?"

"Europe."

"He's not an American?"

"No. He went to school in Switzerland." Laura felt guilty about the omission. She was not ready to break the news to her father that Byron was German. She added enthusiastically, "He's my age."

"Switzerland? How's his English?"

"It's really good."

"Is he Jewish?"

"No. I'm sorry, Dad." She glanced at Byron, who had wandered on foot to the end of the road. She sat down on the curb and stared up at the building across the street. It had a round stained glass window with a Star of David over double bolted doors.

"It's too bad he's not Jewish. Is he with you?"

"Yes."

"That's great. I'm glad you're with someone."

"I know. Thanks, Dad."

"Laura, the ad agency called," her father began. His voice was animated. "Apparently, that hotshot they hired to be your boss didn't work out. There are federal regulations called Sarbanes-Oxley. Your agency, because it is publicly traded, is routinely audited. The new boss didn't have all of his ducks in a row."

"I know about Sarbanes-Oxley. What did he do? Or didn't do?"

"They weren't going to tell me anything. Eventually, I got it out of them that he was bilking the accounts. Boy Wonder couldn't provide documentation for the exorbitant fees the agency was charging the clients. They lost a boatload of money cleaning up after him."

"They said that? Boatload?"

"No. What they said, I am not repeating to you."

Laura chuckled. "Did they tell you how much?"

"They would not give me the exact number. So, after we hung up, I looked up their second-quarter earnings report. It's on the Internet, you know."

"I know, Dad. I was tempted to look . . . "

"It cited an 'unanticipated loss due to Sarbanes-Oxley related expenses.' The stock is at twelve. What was it when you left?"

"Thirty. I was lucky," she added, remembering her stock options. She had had the good timing and judgment to cash in when she did.

"I would say they lost several million. What do you think, Laura?"

"Easily," she said. "The stock devaluation alone is that much, not to mention the fines."

"They had to rent extra offices to house all of the auditors. Imagine having a dozen or so federal inspectors breathing down your neck every day."

"What a disaster."

"That never happened when you were working there."

"No. It did not."

"The Young Turk really screwed up. He's gone now. They want you to come back. They told me they made a big mistake. They said that they should have promoted you instead of hiring that weasel," he said gleefully.

"Is that what they said?" Her father must be embellishing. It was unlike them to be so contrite.

"Yes. I may be paraphrasing their exact words, but yes, that was the gist."

"Wow. I don't know if I'm ready. I just got here."

"What do you mean you just got there? You left in April. It's now July. When are you coming home? It's time to go back to work. You're only forty-five. What will you do when your money runs out? Don't wait until then. Call them now. Do you want the number?"

"I know the number, Dad."

"Call them as soon as we hang up. What time is it where you are?"

"Close to seven."

"It's almost noon here in Chicago. Call them right now. You'll catch them before they leave for lunch."

"Okay, Dad. I'll call."

"Promise?"

"Yes. I promise."

"Good. I love you, Laura."

"I love you, too, Dad."

Laura clicked off the phone and stood up. She became aware of sweat dripping from her armpits. It was caused by work-related stress, a sensation she had not experienced since arriving in Eastern

Europe nearly four months ago. It felt familiar and energizing. She suddenly missed her life in the business world. Laura knew the agency's number by heart. Still, she didn't call.

Her phone rang. It was her dad, again. "I was just about to call," she answered.

"Laura, I forgot to remind you. Tonight is your mother's *yahrtzeit*, "he said, referring to the anniversary of her mom's death.

"I know, Dad."

"What were you planning to do? Is there a synagogue you can go to?"

"Yes. There's a very large one in Budapest." In fact, it was the biggest Jewish house of worship ever built in Europe, according to her guidebook.

"Do they have a service?"

"Yes." Laura had checked into this. "It's not until nine because of *Tisha B'Av*." *Tisha B'Av* was Hebrew for the ninth day of the Jewish month of *Av*, a holiday memorializing the destruction of the First and Second Temples.

"That's right. Your mother died on *Tisha B'Av*. Her *yahrtzeit* is always on *Tisha B'Av*," he lamented, his voice trailing off.

"It's seven years."

"Seven years. You're right. So, are you going?"

"Yes."

"Good. That's my girl." That's my girl. *That's my Laura*. Her father and Byron were beginning to sound like the same person.

After hanging up, Laura grabbed the bicycle. She pedaled toward Byron.

"Hey," she called out as she glided by. "Do you want a lift?" Her pickup line was the single most aggressive thing she had ever said to him.

Braking in front of Byron, she commanded, "Hop on."

Byron mounted the back of the bike. He wrapped his arms around her. Conjuring up all of her brute force, she stood on the pedals and pumped. Her calf and thigh muscles strained. The bicycle wobbled until Laura gained balance and momentum.

"To the Chain Bridge!" she shouted over her shoulder.

"Do you need directions?"

"No. I know how to get there from here."

She was relieved to leave behind (if only for the next hour or so) the hovels and demolition debris of the Jewish Quarter. She imagined that she was a Jewish woman fleeing the German occupation of Hungary. The abysmal truth was that most Jews had not escaped. In the waning days of World War II, the Nazis had herded the Jews from this ghetto to the nearby Chain Bridge, where they summarily shot them to death—mass execution style—and pushed the bodies into the Danube River.

Soon afterwards, the Allies closed in on Berlin and defeated Hitler. For the Nazis, Budapest had been the final hurrah.

A bus backfired and spewed soot at her face. Laura zigzagged through traffic. They came up on a row of riverside hotels and finally the Chain Bridge. It connected urban Pest with the hills and castle of Buda.

They got off the bike and walked with it to the midpoint of the bridge. Her legs ached. Gazing at the ripples of water, Laura wondered what remained of the Jews in the river.

"My father called me," she said.

"Does he want you to come home?"

"Yes. How did you know?"

He smiled. "If I had a daughter, I would not want her running around foreign countries with the likes of me."

"I never told you, I miss the United States."

"Do you want to go back?"

"I have a job offer, president of the advertising agency in Chicago."

"Impressive."

Byron was quiet for several tense seconds, during which Laura feared she was dumping him into the river below. She did not want to do this to him. What was he thinking? And then he said, "I understand that there are artists and art galleries in Chicago."

"There are!"

"If you decide to accept the job, then I will come with you." He added, "If you will have me."

"Yes! Yes! Of course, I will have you." Laura threw her arms around his neck and covered his right cheek with kisses. She feared she was overreacting—he had not, after all, proposed marriage—until he placed his mouth on hers and kissed her deeply and with passion.

When he released her, Laura saw the golden rays of the setting sun reflected on the water. The evening religious service would soon begin.

*

In the suburbs of Chicago, Laura had visited several colossally opulent synagogues, all products of prosperous American Jewry. Nothing she had witnessed had prepared her for the Great Synagogue of Budapest. The stunning temple was constructed in the Byzantine style. Two onion-shaped domes sat atop twin towers. Inside, the size of the nave rivaled the grandest cathedrals of Europe. Rich mosaics adorned the walls and Moorish chandeliers lit the vast interior.

Tourists were everywhere, but Laura had been advised that the service was to take place in the small nearby Heroes' Temple, named for the Hungarian Jews who had served in World War I.

As it was *Tisha B'Av*, the saddest day in Jewish history, there was no conversing among the twenty or so congregants. Everyone was to be silent until the service began. The rabbi was a young woman. She distributed to the attendees flat white candles and sheets of foil. The people sat down on the floor, forming a circle, and shared matches to light the candles. The wax drippings fell on the metallic paper.

It was Byron's first time at a Jewish service. Laura glanced at his profile, which was glowing in the candlelight. *Tisha B'Av*—

though not as intense or celebrated as Yom Kippur, the holiest of holy days of the year—was quite an introduction.

The rabbi spoke from the lectern in Magyar, the Hungarian language. Neither Laura nor Byron knew Magyar. From her fervent tone, Laura sensed that the she was speaking not only of ancient tragedies, but also of the twentieth century genocide of the Jews of Budapest.

This was her seventh *Tisha B'Av* service since her mother had died. She knew from past sermons (in English) that the first Temple had been destroyed due to violent crimes and sexual immorality. The Jews later rebuilt the Temple and no longer committed those sins. Laura recalled one rabbinic interpretation that Jewish infighting had led to the obliteration of the Second Temple, which was never rebuilt. The lesson? That the greatest of all transgressions is hatred.

Tonight this message had a special poignancy for her. Was it possible that a prolonged enmity between Jews and Germans was more sinful than her erotic love for Byron?

The Hungarian rabbi asked them to open up a slim volume, the Hebrew Book of Lamentations. The sorrowful yet enchanting melody had always captivated Laura. This evening was no exception. As in the past, she was moved to sing along softly. She saw Byron gazing at her lovingly and that there were tears in his eyes.

At the conclusion, when everyone repeated the second to the last verse in raised voices and unison, Byron also sang aloud. He followed Laura in Hebrew, one syllable behind her at a time. In English, she knew these words to be:

Turn us to you, O Lord, and we will return.

Renew our days as of old.

Then, all of the worshippers stood up and recited the Mourner's Kaddish, as is customary on *Tisha B'Av*. For Laura, it was also in memory for her mother, who had died on this day. And she cried.

CHAPTER 32:
LEAVE TAKING

The Chicago skyline swooped beneath them. In the blue-gray mist, Laura could make out the iconic structures punctuating the sky and hovering over Lake Michigan. Lake Michigan! An American lake! The Sears Tower! Soon the plane would touch down on the runway and Byron and Laura would step foot onto U.S. soil. She was overcome with joy and wistfulness for her homeland. How patriotic was that?

The last time Laura had occupied any one of those office buildings was the day she had resigned. In the weeks leading up to her decision, her sadistic boss had given her so many assignments that a single hour of free time was a luxury. *His* bosses had reverentially dubbed him The Pit Bull of Chicago. It was a misguided, nostalgic allusion to the legendary Chicago Bulls championship basketball team, led in the 1990s by Michael Jordan. (Must have been from breathing the rarefied air of the board of directors' penthouse suite. Laura would forgive them.)

She recalled a typical Sunday morning: Sitting in a downtown café, sipping a cappuccino, and savoring a melted chocolate chip scone. It had been the equivalent of a spa vacation. Yet even during this brief respite, Laura was plagued with dread. In a few minutes, she would have to go to work. The other, seemingly oblivious people all around her reminded Laura of the haute bourgeoisie of prerevolutionary France. They were leisurely aristocrats. She was, despite her substantial income, of a different class: Wage slavery.

How she had wished to be one of them! Today, from the heights of her jumbo jet window seat and staring down at her hometown, Laura realized that she was one of them and more: In love, valued professionally, and a woman of the world.

Flight 97 to Chicago was filled with the usual complement of ugly Americans. Their mostly overweight bodies were inelegantly pressed into the seats. Laura, with her concave tummy, was an anorexic super model, only at least eight inches too short and about twenty-five years too old. She stared at her thinness underneath the pale yellow floral dress. The ends of her hair were pointed and matted as they grazed the nubby fabric. She sensed that there was a slight odor to her body. She felt distinctly, *dirtily* European and she *loved* it. Her U.S. cohorts had been away on one or two week sojourns. Laura had been on a life-changing journey.

She was not ready for this trip to end.

Gazing up at her boyfriend, she unbuckled both of their seatbelts.

"Laura, we're about to land."

"If I know you, this won't take long."

"You know me very well," he replied. He got out of his aisle seat and took her hand.

They walked up a few rows to the bulkhead where there was a lavatory. A male flight attendant stood in the nearby kitchen galley, but his back was turned to Laura and Byron. They both pushed into the small bathroom.

It was a tight fit! How did the airlines expect just one person, let alone two, to manage in such minuscule quarters?

Laura and Byron were crammed in on three sides, toilet, door, and sink. They quickly unzipped his trousers and lifted up her dress.

As usual, he was steely hard and she was slippery wet. He hoisted her above the much-used basin so that her legs and butt hung over it in midair. Her back was pressed against the streaked and fogged mirror. He plowed into her, whereupon she felt a second rigid object prod her. It must be the faucet! Just then, water gushed up and soaked the back of her dress.

The fountain splashed their bare thighs. Byron reached his arms around her, grasping her ribcage. The more he pushed into her, the more the water spurted. It drenched them as they both climaxed.

The plane landed on the runway with a thud. They giggled and collapsed against one another. They had made it.

Laura began to move the door latch, about to exit the cramped, flooded compartment. He stopped her, lowering her hand. He tenderly held her damp face.

"Let's wait for the cattle to get off the plane, shall we?"

"Good idea," she replied, also visualizing a stampede of passengers grappling with oversized carry-on bags.

"Whatever happens out there, on American soil, you know I love you."

What did he mean by that? It sounded ominous. "I love you, too."

They kissed one final time. Laura held on to him for as long as possible, as if saying goodbye to the Old World. They pushed open the lavatory door.

Stepping off the plane and into the tube connecting to the terminal, Laura felt the steamy Midwestern humidity that leaked through the cracks. It was the oppressive, stifling summer heat. Chicago! America!

At U.S. Customs, Homeland Security agents separated them as if they were at Auschwitz. Laura breezed through the checkpoint. Byron was directed to wait in a different, long, and creeping line. *This is O'Hare*, Laura reminded herself. *Here, a citizen who happens to be Jewish receives preferential treatment to any foreigner.*

Next, they proceeded outside to the loading zone to get a cab. It was the early evening. They had gained seven hours. Their driver was an African American female. Her headdress and caftan shimmered with golden threads. She effortlessly threw their bags into the trunk.

A sister! Laura could barely contain her excitement. She had not encountered someone so richly real to her in months. Hallelujah! Hallelujah! A gospel chorus was hollering in her head.

"How y'all doin'?" The woman turned to greet them from the front seat of the cab. Her face was radiant and her teeth were beaming white. *There is nothing better than this,* thought Laura. *Well . . . almost nothing.*

"Great! It feels *great* to be in the United States," Laura answered with unbridled enthusiasm.

"I've never been out of this country. Do you believe that, girl? Not even to Canada."

"Hey, that's cool. Why bother? Right?"

Laura glanced over at Byron, to make sure that she had not just offended him with this comment. Apparently not. He was smiling at the female bonding.

"Not even to freakin' *Wisconsin.* I don't know. Maybe I'm missing something?"

"Maybe just a little." Laura tilted her head in the direction of Byron so that the driver could see in the rearview mirror that she meant *him.*

"Hmm, I *see* what you mean."

Laura took in a deep breath. Despite the evident pollutants, the American air smelled pure. The land of the free!

The radio dial was set to WHPK, the station of Laura's alma mater, the University of Chicago. It was the nightly jazz program from seven to nine p.m. Bluesy music filled the taxi as they sped on the expressway. A songstress was wailing about a lying and cheating man.

Laura leaned back and let the wind whip her face. The sky was darkening and the white headlamps from the oncoming cars zipped past them.

"Just like the Autobahn," Byron remarked. "Are you happy to be home, *Geliebte?*"

"Oh, yes! I am."

"Good. I am happy to be here, too."

CHAPTER 33:
THE FINAL CONFRONTATION

"What fresh hell is this?"

The Dorothy Parker quote kept reverberating in Laura's mind. Her German boyfriend was the son of a Nazi. They were about to meet her dad. As a twelve-year-old boy, during World War II, he had run civil defense messages. At the same time, across the Atlantic Ocean, Byron's father was partaking in drills with the Hitler Youth. What fresh irony was that?

Both young men had come of age in the Age of "The Final Solution." Now, Laura felt that she was entering into the warzone of "The Final Confrontation." It would end with one of her loved ones banished from her life forever.

Her father would surely have an as strong or a stronger negative reaction to Byron's parentage than she had. He was never going to tolerate such an entanglement for his one and only daughter. There was no way. While she did not expect him to issue an ultimatum—"Either the Nazi goes or I go!"—Laura was certain that their relationship would never be the same. Whereas there had always been warmth between them, Laura foresaw a new and permanent frost.

If she was lucky! Her father was going be devastated. In high school, he had tried to prohibit her from seeing Christian boys. For dating the son of a Nazi, he may very well disown her. How could she do this to him? How could she do this to herself? Would he say Kaddish for her? Would he grieve for her as if she were dead?

What if the news killed him first? Laura would never forgive herself.

She was going to lose her nerve before making it to the restaurant.

They were cosseted in the leather confines of her Cadillac CTS.

Laura had deferred to the wishes of her father when making this purchase. Not only had he urged her to buy American, he had advocated this specific make and model. Why?

"If, G-d forbid, you are ever in an accident, you'll crush the other car."

"Dad! How can you say that?"

He laughed and then repeated, "G-d forbid." It was typical of him to put her on a pedestal. While Laura had willingly given up owning a BMW, it would be a true sacrifice to forgo her Bavarian lover.

Byron remarked, "Nice car, *Geliebte.*"

"Thanks." Please don't call me that. Please don't call me *Geliebte*, Laura wanted to say. No German. Not in front of my father.

She had misled him into thinking that Byron was Swiss. Switzerland had been a neutral country during World War II. Her dad might not find fault with the country known for holey cheese and tax evading bank accounts.

And yet: "If you're not with us, you're against us." George Bush had uttered these words when declaring the War on Terror. Laura knew that her father held this same view regarding the Holocaust. Hence, Switzerland, neutral or otherwise, was unsafe territory. Even FDR had turned his back on the Jews in peril in Europe, prior to the Japanese attack on Pearl Harbor. Turning away is turning against. In this context, Laura wholeheartedly agreed.

She felt like she was emotionally drowning. She was ten feet underwater in a pool and the chlorine was stinging her eyes. These were acidic, not salty tears. As slaves in Egypt, the Jews had also shed bitter tears, according to the Passover story.

She had not been behind the wheel in months. Panic, confusion, and dread overwhelmed her. She pulled over to the side of the road.

"I'm sorry. I can't do this. I can't introduce you to my father." The words were tumbling out, uncontrollably and unedited. "I know you came all the way from Europe to be with me, but I can't be with you. I can't. I'm sorry." She burst into tears.

He put his arms around her and held her while she sobbed into his blazer. "Don't worry, Laura. I'll take care of everything. You'll see."

"How?"

"Here." He handed her a clean white handkerchief. She indelicately blew into it.

"I don't understand."

"I have my ways."

Laura looked at him skeptically. She wiped the tears from her eyes and checked her reflection in the rear view mirror. Unbelievably, her makeup was untouched. She restarted the engine and drove off.

The restaurant was in the same town where Laura had grown up. Then, the population had largely consisted of highly assimilated, affluent Jews. The major change in the area was the recent and constant influx of the religious Hasidim.

The dining room upholstery was a muted salmon color. The tablecloths, a pure white. Pale brown hardwood flooring was polished to a high sheen. The decorative colors reminded Laura of the traditional Jewish Sunday morning meal of bagels, lox, and cream cheese. Wall sconces and fine tableware helped to create an atmosphere of understated elegance.

Everyone—from the mature waiters and waitresses, to the parking valet, from the busboys to the owner—knew her dad. As well they should. He had been coming here for decades.

She spotted her father with his girlfriend at one of the round tables for four. When he saw her, he stood up and began smiling from ear to ear. He looked so happy to see her!

For her part, Laura was thrilled to see him. He took her head in his hands and kissed her on both of her cheeks. It was far more expressive than the cordial gesture between two European acquaintances. They both started to cry. Their emotional reunion momentarily eclipsed Byron and Paula. While Laura enjoyed basking in his lavish attention, she felt obliged to break the spell. She stepped back. Paula was looking at them impatiently.

"Aren't you going to introduce us to your new boyfriend?"

"Yes, of course. This is Byron!"

Paula stood up to shake Byron's hand. "Hello, Byron. I'm Paula."

Why did she have to jump in like that before her father had properly greeted Byron? It was typical of her. She was always so pushy.

She watched her dad as he gazed at Byron. The wide grin was pasted on his face, yet Laura detected his anxiety. Maybe Paula had moved in to give her dad a few seconds to adjust to the new man in her life.

It had always been like this. Her father had in the past displayed discomfort in the presence of her boyfriends. It had made sense when Laura was a teenager and even in college. But now?

Byron began, "It is a pleasure to meet you, Mr. Levine."

Laura winced. His German accent was so blatant! How had she ever mistaken him for British? She accidentally glanced at Paula, who knowingly raised an eyebrow. Laura was impressed that she could do this given her Botox injections.

"Nice meeting you, too," said her dad, relaxing a bit. He seemed oblivious to Byron's Gestapo-like tone. The two men shook hands. "Thank you for taking care of my daughter."

Laura registered that remark as a test, which each of her poor, clueless ex-boyfriends had failed miserably:

Are you serious? I don't need to take care of Laura. She takes care of me.

This is 1999. Your daughter is an independent woman. That's why I love her.

You're welcome. I think. What did Laura tell you?

Present day Laura braced herself for Byron's reply.

"It was—and is—my absolute delight to take care of Laura."

Her dad beamed. "I completely agree with you!"

All four took their seats around the table. The waiter approached them. "Good evening, Sirs. *Mesdames.*" He placed menus in front of them. A busboy filled their goblets with water.

Laura was having déjà vu. She hearkened back to the dinner in Berlin with the elder *Herr* Baumgaarten. Byron seemed calmer now than he had been with his own papa. He was smiling eagerly as he read the menu. *He's delusional,* thought Laura. *Just wait until the firestorm hits.*

"I am going to have the matzo ball soup and the beef brisket," Byron announced.

"I'll have the same thing. I don't even need to look at the menu." Her father chuckled. "Only you forgot the *zsimis,* Byron."

"Plus the *zsimis,*" Byron added, using the Yiddish word for sweet potatoes coated in brown sugar.

How did he know so much about Jewish food? Had he done preparatory research?

"I'm ordering the stuffed cabbage, just to be different from the two of you," Paula said. "What are you having, Laura? The giant German knockwurst?"

Laura threw her a sharp look. She *knew.*

"Go ahead," said Paula. "Eat whatever you want. All the meat here is Kosher."

"I'll have what they're having."

After the waiter took their orders, Paula said to Byron, "You seem to know a lot about Jewish food."

"My mother was a wonderful cook."

"Was you mother Jewish?"

Laura fretted. Why must Paula goad him?

"In Germany, you never know," replied Byron.

Laura was shocked by his quick and free admission.

"You're German?" Her father was visibly stunned.

"Yes."

Paula smiled slyly. "I never would have guessed. You seem so . . . "

" . . . British?" Laura interrupted. "Doesn't he? That's what I thought, too, when I met him."

Her father studied Byron. "A lot of Jews in Germany changed their religion to escape persecution. If your mother was born Jewish, then you know what that means?"

"That I'm Jewish?"

"You could be. In Judaism, the child always takes on the religion of the mother."

"That's because you always know who your mother is," explained Paula. "The father, he could be anyone."

"And that is the tradition of our people." Her father flashed another brilliant smile.

DNA testing notwithstanding, thought Laura.

"There is hope for me." Byron smiled back at them and took Laura's hand. "You never know."

"You never know," Paula said, drawing out the words, teasingly.

"You never know," Laura joined in.

Her dad grew serious. "Tell us about your father."

"The father who might not be your father," interjected Paula. Laura marveled that she did not even need wine to act this way.

Byron began, "There is a part of him that will always be a mystery to me. I must admit to you, I am deeply ashamed, he was a German soldier in World War II."

"My father, Laura's grandfather, was an American soldier in World War I. He fought with the Allies in France." He turned to Paula. "You knew that, didn't you, honey?"

"Yes, I did. You've told me many times."

"Your side clobbered the Germans, which led to disillusion in our society, Hitler, and the Nazis . . . " Byron's voice trailed off. Tears were in his eyes. "Sir, I am so, so sorry."

They fell into a long moment of quietude, anguish, and reverence. It was disturbed, finally, by the waiter bringing over three bowls of matzo ball soup.

Laura sliced her matzo ball with the edge of her tablespoon and paused for the steaming broth to cool. "He saved the life of a

Jewish girl," she said.

"Who did?"

"Byron's father."

"A rather specious claim on his part . . . "

"What do you mean, Byron? He told us the whole story when we met him for dinner. You should have heard it, Dad. It was an incredibly detailed account. It could have been a scene from a movie, like *Schindler's List."*

"Indeed," said Byron. "It was 'pitch perfect,' intended to reel you in emotionally, which is precisely why I thought he was lying. In the more than sixty years since the war, he never once talked about his experiences. Why now? Why tell you? And who is this Jewish girl? 'Tatiana'? Is that even a Jewish name?"

"Taschi—what? It sounds *goyisha* to me." Paula was employing the Yiddish word for non-Jewish.

"Tatiana," Laura said. "She was from Kiev. A lot of Jews were. He loved her. Are you saying that none of this is true? Why don't you believe him?"

"I know my papa. He can be quite the showman."

"You can give him some credit, Laura. Either he is a true hero or he went to the trouble of making up a story to help put you at ease," her dad said.

"To take out some of the sting of meeting a Nazi," Paula added.

"More likely," Byron rejoined, "to keep you from wanting to kill him."

"Yeah, that too. Definitely, that too," said her dad. Her father and her boyfriend were nodding in agreement.

"Anyway," Paula said, reaching for the breadbasket. "I don't know what all the fuss is about. He's Byron's papa. He's not Byron."

"Paula's right," said her dad. "Try the soup, Laura. It's delicious."

Laura was astonished. That was it? It had taken her father all of ten minutes to arrive at this self-evident truth whereas she had struggled for months with the dilemma. Laura suspected that the meeting would have gone differently had her dad's girlfriend not been there to move things along. She was surprisingly indebted to the "Be True to The Beauty of You" Paula for the role she had just played in The Final Confrontation.

Her father was accepting Byron! It was a miracle to be celebrated! Uncork the champagne! Or at least, bring out the . . .

" . . . Manischewitz!" Her father completed her thought, out loud. "Byron, I hope you will join us in the drinking of Kosher wine."

"I am honored."

"You must be forewarned," said Laura. "It is really sweet."

"That's what makes it great. Like you." He winked at her.

Her dad beckoned the restaurant maitre d'. "Please bring us four glasses of Manischewitz."

The maitre d' returned with a small entourage. The busboy placed four wineglasses beside their place settings. The waiter poured the deep purple liquid.

As glasses were raised, the employees lingered and watched over the table. They seemed to sense that something wondrous was about to occur.

In first grade Hebrew School, Laura had memorized in Hebrew several essential blessings. The first was over the wine, at six years old and well under drinking age. The second was over the bread (known as the *Motzi*). There were others, for lighting the Shabbat and Chanukah candles. The most challenging to recite was her favorite. It was called "the *Shechyanu*." Its purpose was to thank G-d for sustaining and enabling us to reach this special day.

Her father said the short Hebrew blessing, which extolled the Creator of the fruit of the vine. At the end, he stared at Laura while uttering one final word, "Amen." He pronounced it "aw-mane" as was the Eastern European, Old World custom. Laura had been schooled in the New Hebrew, the modern day language used in Israel. She simultaneously said "ah-mane" to her father's "aw-mane." It was her usual token of daughterly defiance, which her dad routinely attempted to drown out.

"Aw-mane!" shouted Byron.

"That settles it," said Laura. "Now we know whose side you're on."

The four of them clinked together their glasses and drank up.

Byron again raised his glass. "I would like to propose . . . "

" . . . a toast," completed Laura.

"No, *Geliebte,*" he said, using the German term for lover. "Not a toast."

"Then what?" asked Paula.

"I would like to propose . . . " He turned to her dad. " . . . Marriage to your daughter," Byron said.

Laura was at once shocked, hopeful, and ecstatic.

"Given my legacy, I will understand if you say no."

Please, please. Don't let him say no.

"If you say yes, I will be eternally grateful."

Seven years ago, at a much more sorrowful time, her father had told her that the happiest day of his life had been when he had married her mother. Laura did not have to imagine this. Laura knew. She had seen the black and white, blown-up wedding photo of her mom feeding her dad a huge wedge of cake . . .

Her father looked just as happy today as he had then.

He replied, "I never thought I'd see . . . "

"I know you didn't, honey." Paula laughed.

Laura knew what he had been about to say. A tremendous weight was being lifted from him.

"What do *you* say, Laura?" her father asked.

"I say . . . yes!"

At which point, there was much kissing and hugging of the bride and groom to be, a round of bubbly, and a buoyant reading of "The *Shechyanu.*" Everyone in the restaurant joined in, thanking G-d for this amazing day.

Later that night after making love for the first time in her Chicago bed, Laura gazed out the window that extended from floor to ceiling of her high-rise condo. A pancake moon shone over the Great Lake Michigan. "Look, Byron. It's a Bohemian moon."

"What is a Bohemian moon, my *Geliebte*? Is this another one of your advertising slogans? I suppose I will have to start getting used to them."

"Sure," she improvised. "'Travel to Eastern Europe. Under a Bohemian moon, you will find your way.'"

A new adventure had begun.

About the Author

Does Lilou DuPont visit Eastern Europe in order to research settings *or* does she write about Eastern Europe as an excuse to travel there? Lilou studied erotic writing at The New School in New York. She grew up in Connecticut and lives in Washington, DC, where she enjoys a successful career in advertising. *Dangerous Love* is her first novel.

In the mood for more Crimson Romance? Check out *Ruby's Reward* by Alicia Thorne at *CrimsonRomance.com*.

www.ingramcontent.com/pod-product-compliance
Lightning Source LLC
Chambersburg PA
CBHW010637100726
47900CB00011B/2864

* 9 7 8 1 4 4 0 5 5 4 1 0 0 *